Harlequin Romances

OTHER
Harlequin Romances
by JOYCE DINGWELL

Inland Paradise

by

JOYCE DINGWELL

Harlequin Books

TORONTO • LONDON • NEW YORK • AMSTERDAM • SYDNEY • WINNIPEG

Original hardcover edition published in 1976
by Mills & Boon Limited

ISBN 0-373-02047-3

Harlequin edition published February 1977

Printed in U.S.A.

CHAPTER ONE

EXCEPT for the carefully snipped-out advertisement, underlined in red ink and pinned securely to Joanne's letter to
Georgina so Georgina could not possibly miss it, nothing
would have happened. Nothing, that is, except Georgina
returning to Sydney as she had decided she would have to;
finding a bed-sit, finding a job, living the life she didn't
want to live but reluctantly had accepted as inevitable now
that her stepfather was dead.

But the advertisement changed everything, though no
doubt Joanne hadn't had that in mind when she got to work
with scissors and red ink. More likely Joanne's lip had been
curling and she had wished the scissors she was plying
could be put to more telling work, for example on
Georgina. Yes, Georgina smiled ruefully, between the two
of them things were like that.

Joanne and Georgina were stepsisters, and Georgina's
stepfather was—sorrowfully for Georgina it was 'had been'
now—Joanne's father. Lucky Joanne to have had a father
like that!

The marriage between Georgina's mother and Joanne's
father had been an ideal one, but their respective daughters
never had 'jelled'. The two girls had had different outlooks
as children, avoided each other as teenagers, and as young
women ... Well, as Georgina confided now to the snipped-
out, underlined advertisement, the balloon had gone up.

Gone up, to be exact, last week, when Joanne had flown
from Sydney to this obscure outpost at the back of Bourke
to decide what to do with her father's effects.

Joanne had sat in the cramped caravan on the edge of the

outpost—the other edge touched the mulga—and said incredulously: 'But Dad must have had more than this.'

'He didn't, Joanne. He was working for himself, remember. His findings weren't commissioned or anything like that.'

'What was he working on?'

'Permian occurrences in rock, cosmic rays, attention to possible nickel "signs", general geo stuff aimed for the next geophysical year,' Georgina supplied.

'Spare me the dreary rest!' An estimating silence. 'How far had he gone with the book? It was a book, I take it?'

'Yes, a book.'

'How far?'

'Halfway.'

'Can you finish it?'

'Of course not. I was the bottle-washer here, not the collaborator,' Georgina admitted frankly.

'All the same, you must have picked up a lot of gen.'

'I did. But I'm not a graduate. Why, I wasn't even a scholar.'

'Oh,' Joanne had smiled thinly, 'I remember that.' Another contemplative pause. 'So you don't think you can take it to the end, find a publisher?'

'And hand you the money, Joanne? No,' Georgina had said tightly, for the idea of finishing Stepfather's work had occurred, not with Joanne in mind, but as a tribute to the dear old man she had adored. In fact she had even——

At once, in the shrewd way she always had been able to read Georgina's mind, Joanne had read it now.

'You *have* been thinking along those lines, you sly puss!'

'No.'

'Oh, come off it, Georgina, you're as transparent as glass. You're deceiving me—Dad's work *is* valuable and you intend to grab it for yourself.'

'It isn't valuable in its present form and it would take a lot of money and a lot of brains to make it saleable.'

'That would leave you out on both counts,' Joanne had

said acidly. 'Then why did you want his notes?'

'I didn't say I did.'

'No, but I can tell. Well, you can have them ... at a price. I can't be bothered looking for a buyer. He would have to be some professor, anyway, and academics are always very dull and usually hard-up. You can pay me——' She arrived at a sum.

'Now,' she had continued, 'let's get down to tangibles. The caravan, to begin with. How much will it bring?'

'Not much out here, there's nobody to buy it. We're the west, admittedly, but New South Wales west, not the fabled "inside". Not' ... and Georgina's thoughts drifted a moment ... 'the Mirage Country.' The Mirage Country, she thought wistfully, for Stepfather had often enchanted her with his descriptions of the centre. His mirage accounts had been both scientific and romantic, for that had been typical of Stepfather. 'An appearance of scenes owing to the varying layers of hot or cold air,' he had said in one breath, then: 'Pictures plucked from one garden to blossom in another.' Georgina had preferred the second account. To her mirages were the stuff of dreams.

'What difference does location make?' Joanne had demanded crossly.

'The difference of big finds to little or even none at all,' Georgina sighed, 'that's what I'm trying to point out to you, Joanne. The bulk of the prospectors, meaning possible caravan purchasers, are now out there, not here. There's nothing doing here.'

'But surely there must be someone passing through and wanting to try their hand before they move on? They'd have to stop somewhere, and though this is as poor as they could get, it's still a shelter of sorts. And everyone knows' ... before Georgina could repeat herself about there being nothing doing ... 'that you have only to dig a hole and something pops up.'

'Not in this part of the west any longer. None of the holes are popping,' Georgina had said emphatically. 'Even the one store is closing up, and the hotel's swing doors have swung for the last time.'

Joanne had grimaced, remarked distastefully that she didn't wonder about that, then advised Georgina to get what she could for the van.

'Also cash in on all the equipment. Those instruments, books, microscopes . . . oh, yes, and the typewriter.'

Georgina stiffened. 'The typewriter is mine, Joanne.'

'So you say.'

'It is. I sent for and paid for it.'

'Out of savings from free keep!'

'Well, what else did you expect from me? I looked after your father while he worked. I went out with him after specimens, I wrote up his findings. I recorded his views. I loved doing it, and I'm not complaining, for the best year of my life was that year with Stepfather, but still I wasn't paid.'

'In which case you're claiming the typewriter?'

. . . The bike and sidecar, too, Georgina could have added, for they had acquired a secondhand outfit, and Georgina had driven, and Stepfather had bounced in the sidecar, for biking now was the accepted method of getting over the desert, and prospectors as well as stockmen were mechanised nowadays.

'The typewriter must be sold,' Joanne had proclaimed, stonily dismissing Georgina's claim, 'and all the proceeds sent down.' She had marked the details in a book.

Over tea—Georgina felt sorely tempted to charge Joanne for it—Joanne had said:

'I wouldn't be going on like this, of course, if Father had left me anything. But all he had went on your mother.'

That had been untrue as well as unkind. There *had* been money spent on her mother, Georgina remembered that sadly, but it had been Mother's money originally, not Stepfather's. Stepfather had been kind, lovable and loved . . . but he had never been successful. Georgina had started to remind his daughter of this, then stopped. What did it

8

matter now? she had thought.

Joanne had finished her notes in her little black book; she accepted a second cup of tea, then looked at her step-sister appraisingly.

'And what are your plans now?' she asked patronisingly.

'No plans. What plans could I have?'

'Quite true.' There was a little lift to Joanne's lip as she scrutinised Georgina. So brown. So open-faced. So—well, corn-fed. So—yes, *plain*. Also doing nothing about it, that is if anything could be done about it, which Joanne strongly doubted.

'But what will you *do*?' she had asked. 'If this place is folding up, you can't stay here.'

'I couldn't even if Windmill Junction was busy. Who would want me? Your father did, but he was different. I've not graduated, I have a good smattering of geology, but I still haven't the necessary degrees.'

'Then women do come west?' Joanne had yawned; she wasn't really interested.

'For the bigger companies, yes, if they have brains, yet even then very seldom. Men are preferred out here.'

'If something big started up, you could cook, perhaps.' Joanne's tone was still patronising.

'I would rush at it,' Georgina had admitted honestly, not minding the patronage. 'I would do the humblest task, the most menial job to stay in the west. This is my life and this is my kind of country, and it's going to shatter me leaving it.' She had stopped abruptly, aware that she had done something she had never done with her stepsister: she had bared her soul. Perhaps, she had thought a little wistfully, it would break up something, bring them closer together . . .

A little low amused laugh from Joanne had spiked that idea.

'You have peculiar tastes, Georgina,' she drawled. 'To me these sorts of places are the utter ends of the earth. I simply can't wait to get into my car and head south again. South to civilisation. Just look at that scene.' She had indi-

9

cated the terrain beyond the narrow window of the small caravan, and Georgina had looked with her.

'Hell,' Joanne had pronounced.

'It's the way you see it, Joanne.'

'All that dry old mulga, brittle as bones and ready to snap off! Sticks and stones and horrible beasties like snakes and lizards and dragons and goannas. Everything tough, everything bare, everything bleached or washed out.'

'Not when the sun hits the rocks; it's Arabian Nights then,' Georgina contradicted.

'Sand everywhere. It's even in this tea.'

'Odd though it may seem to you I think it's beautiful. I love it and I'll be unhappy to go.'

'Well, don't let sentiment delay you. I need the money. I'll leave now, Georgina, I want to get somewhere decent for the night—if there are any decent places out here. I'll write from Sydney to see how you've done with the sale. And don't go getting any ideas about cheating me, or taking out a commission, for I'll be on the alert.' Joanne rose. 'Thanks for the tea.'

'Sand and all?'

'I suppose you don't taste it. Your twelve months here have made a positive barbarian of you, Georgina, a real primitive.'

'Are females barbarians? Primitives?'

'Presumably if the males are. Anyway, you're *not*, are you?' Joanne was almost talking to herself.

'Not barbarian?' echoed Georgina.

'Not female. Look at your cropped hair and brown skin. No moisturiser, not even any lipstick. You're—why, you're a "feller".' Joanne gave her disagreeable laugh. 'George, not Georgina, should be the name. And yet' ... not giving Georgina a chance to defend herself ... 'the poor "boy" has his feelings. He actually *likes* this godforsaken hole.'

'No, Joanne, I love it.'

'Then it was bad news for you, wasn't it, when Father died?' Her stepsister's voice was light.

'Very bad.'

'For you have to leave,' Joanne had continued, 'as I'm leaving now.' This time she really did make a move, and within minutes her car had driven off.

The letter—with the advertisement—had arrived a week later. Georgina had picked it up in the town. She was surprised that Joanne had written so promptly, and then she saw the enclosure and knew why. Typically, Joanne hadn't been able to resist another jab at her stepsister.

'Dear G, This caught my attention, so I am sending it on to you. "If only", I can hear you moan, "I was a man!" If I could help at all by issuing a reference that you are— almost, I would do so willingly. Remember how I said you should be George instead? But alas, employers need more than stepsisterly advice. How is the sale proceeding? Don't hurry it if it means less money, but on the other hand don't spread it out. I can't wait too long. Best of luck with this job application if you decide to try it; I'm sure, even though you're not a scholar, you could handle the post like a man. Goodbye now, George—Joanne.'

Georgina put the letter down. Pig, she had thought, as she had thought ever since she was twelve and had been told by her mother that she now had a sister the same age.

'Joanne has golden curls and violet eyes and I'm sure you'll love her,' Mother had said uncertainly.

Georgina (straight khaki hair, khaki eyes) had liked the golden curls and the violet eyes—but disliked Joanne.

Well, that was all water under the bridge now, and the things that Joanne had done to her since, the mean little things, the sly, covetous incidents, had rippled away with the water. So whatever it was that Joanne had sent now could mean nothing worse.

Then Georgina read it, and knew at once that she couldn't possibly pass it over; not even dismiss it as Joanne had said, with a moan that she was not a male.

It was an advertisement in the *Sydney Morning Herald*: a Positions Vacant ad. It read:

'Young man wanted to assist in general exploration work; some mineral and geological knowledge welcome, an acceptance of cattle advisable since location is on a cattle station, but most of all common sense essential. Ability to ride motorcycle an advantage, also to fend for self, as cabin provided is secluded and away from homestead. Successful applicant if a student would have ample time for study as actual work would be only intermittent. Enthusiasm necessary, good health essential, and a tolerance of the inland very important. Apply——'

There followed a telephone number, by the figures a Sydney connection. After the number there was a name and a place; the name was Roper, and the place was Lucy River.

The Lucy River! The Big Lucy! Lucy had been another of Stepfather's 'enchantments', that is enchantments for Georgina. Stepfather had worked up there once and had done a paper on his findings, and his explanations as to how a river could grow from sixty yards to sixty miles, as with his account of mirages, had been both scientific and romantic, both practical and yet the stuff of dreams.

Georgina dreamed now as she re-read the advertisement that Joanne had sent in contempt.

Young man wanted.

If only, she moaned, and Joanne would have chalked up a success, I were a man instead!

She slept on it ... only she didn't, not really, for she was awake for more than half the night. The Mirage Country, she kept on turning over and over in her mind, the Lucy River. Big Lucy, that could rise in a few hours to an inland sea. How could anyone sleep when they thought of that?

She thought next of Sydney, mean, hurried, dusty and discouraged as all big cities are now, under washed-out, grey-daubed skies. She thought of typing, not jumping on to her motorcycle and going out to look for 'signs' or for gossans, putting coloured ribbons on the finds so she could

12

go back to them the next day.

She thought of mornings, new as mornings in cities are never new. She thought of the violets and reds and terracottas that the west, even only as far as the back of Bourke, puts on at evening.

Most of all she thought again of the Mirage Country, of Big Lucy; Lucy shrinking to a few feet in the Dry, then in the Wet spreading as far as the eye could stretch.

I can't, she told the little caravan, I *can't* go back to the coast.

She was bleary-eyed at dawn, and just as it had been when she had been a child, emotion robbed her of her voice. But that wasn't going to stop her, she was still going to apply. By phone. There had been no indication on the advertisement as to what date it had been lodged, so Georgina was taking no risk with time; she would telephone at once. That she had no voice didn't deter her, either. She would stand beside Bill at the store and prompt him in every word.

Bill ran the last remaining business in Windmill Junction, a petrol station outside and an emporium within. At least an emporium had been intended, though a trading post had eventuated, and now even that was breaking up. Bill listened to Georgina's hoarse proposal without enthusiasm until Georgina picked up a pair of smallish boots he was stuck with, and promised to buy them if he would—if——

While Bill turned over the proposition, Georgina looked around her and knew the same magic as she had when she had first arrived here at Windmill. Who on earth could not be enchanted with a frontier town store?

The unbelievable confusion still intoxicated her ... the muddled dress materials, the toppling tins of fruit, the billycans, the rugs, the ties, the ten-gallon hats, the perfumes. Bacon hung from rafters, and there was a solemn sausage that Bill wiped over every day with a damp rag. There were handkerchiefs, fish paste, chocolates that lost their colour

13

at once, and strawberry jam.

'Dunno,' demurred Bill, but Georgina knew he wanted to make sure of his boot sale. Those smaller boots had certainly hung fire, and the way things were now ... She put down the money and whispered huskily to him:

'I'll dial, listen, then write down for you what I want you to say.'

'All right,' said Bill.

Georgina dialled and connected almost at once. When the voice came from Sydney it was very clear, but she shuddered to think what the sound from this end must be. Bill's store was never a silent refuge and now that he was selling out it had become a rowdy market.

She scribbled down:

'I'm ringing concerning your ad.'

Bill recited it.

'Oh yes,' said the male voice from Sydney ... no, drawled, really ... 'it's still open.'

'I'm speaking for a lady.' Again Bill followed Georgina's writing.

'A *what*?' shouted the voice quite violently, no drawl now.

Georgina scrawled:

'A lady. She has all the qualifications and she's interested.'

Bill complied.

'Then tell her,' said the Sydney voice very distinctly, 'no go. I am *not* interested. I don't want a female. Do you get that?'

Georgina wrote urgently:

'Please let me explain.'

Bill mouthed it.

'No woman. Final.'

To make sure of it, the receiver at the other end went definitely down. Down with a bang.

'What else, Georgina?' asked Bill.

'Nothing,' Georgina whispered bleakly.

14

'Bad luck, but you'll still buy the boots?'

'Yes, Bill.' Georgina paid up. Then a thought struck her. 'I'll also buy a writing pad.'

'Thanks, Georgina.'

'And an envelope and stamp.'

'I can even supply you a postman,' Bill grinned, 'there's a character going through tonight, and if you'd like to pen your message now he'd post it in Sydney.'

Georgina did, only she typed, not penned, it. She had brought the typewriter in with the intention of selling it, and now she blessed its unrevealing print, for she had, she knew, a distinctly un-male hand. It was a bit of luck, too, losing her voice, she thought as she straightened the paper in preparation; for if the ruse did come off, he, that man, wouldn't be able to remember her, since she had not spoken a word, only written down what Bill had to say. Though, as Joanne would no doubt have scornfully pointed out, Georgina's was a deep, rather husky male tone, no feminine trill.

She ran her tongue over her lips. She must make good sense. If she didn't, she grinned privately, it could be put down to the atmosphere of a frontier store, to bacon, lingerie, dolls, boxes of rivets and a crowd of big brown bargaining men all mixed up together. Rowdily together.

'Dear Sir,' she duly began.

'I hereby apply,' she tapped on, undeterred by the noise and by Bill telling her to step on it as the 'postman' was leaving, 'for your job. I am not yet a mining graduate, but I do have a good working knowledge of what you appear to require, and also I like cattle. I am young and can ride a cycle, and I can fend for myself. I am working on a thesis' ... well, Stepfather's uncompleted book in a way was a thesis ... 'and I have a lot of common sense. I am enthusiastic, I have good health, and as you see from my address, Windmill Junction, I am tolerant of inland conditions.

'Assuring you of my good faith,

'George Brown.'

Well, she thought, Joanne had called her that, declared her to be George and not Georgina.

She put the letter in the envelope, typed the address, applied the stamp. The 'character' took it from her, and he must have made good time going south, for a wire came for Georgina three days after, and that, for Windmill Junction, was as fleet as sound.

The tone of the wire was genial; even the promise of a friendship sounded in it. Evidently this Roper person had no objection to men.

'The job is yours, Mr Brown,' announced the telegram. 'You appear the right type, even though only one other applicant got in touch—a woman. Definitely no woman apart from my housekeeper allowed here. Find your way to Roper's, Lucy River. Mrs Willmott will brief you. I will be away for several weeks yet. Looking forward to a good association. L. Roper.'

'I reckon,' said Bill, looking at the length of the wire, 'at what the post office is charging these days, that bloke must be on the right side of the ledger, Georgina.'

'I reckon so, too,' Georgina smiled back. She could have added: 'But so am I, Bill.'

For though she was leaving here she was not going back to Sydney; instead she was going to Stepfather's country, the fabled Mirage Country, the Lucy River country where water could spread from sixty yards to sixty miles overnight. She was going to desert that could break your heart one day then fill it with joy the next day, to sand and gibber and everything dead that could change before your eyes to grass and flowers.

I think, thought Georgina, almost achingly happy, that although I haven't been there before, I'm going home.

16

CHAPTER TWO

IT took Georgina three days to wind up her stepfather's, now Joanne's, affairs. The amount she managed to coax out of the Windmill Junctioneers was so meagre that she knew Joanne would be enraged, but as the locals were all as she was, getting ready to move on, she couldn't blame them for not wanting to buy; or if they did buy for giving as little as possible, as they would probably have to leave the loot behind when they finally took off. Under the circumstances she considered that Joanne had been lucky to sell anything at all.

She had decided to defy her stepsister and retain the typewriter. If she finally got into the employ of Mr Roper of Lucy River (and the more she thought about *that*, the less resolved she became) she would need the machine for his reports. Her writing, if not her deep voice, would give her away at once. As soon as she was settled wherever Fate decided her to settle, she would drop a line to Joanne and tell her she would start paying her so-called debts from any salary she received. Joanne was not entitled to the money, but it was the easiest way out.

The caravan, she soon found out, was a white elephant. No one wanted a shabby little caravan; these days the prospectors went in for fitted motor vans, for the roads were bad enough for four wheels, let alone more wheels again that had to be towed behind.

Disheartened after putting it to a dozen sympathetic but hard-up prospectors, suddenly it came to Georgina. Bill. Good old Bill.

'But I don't want a caravan, Georgina,' Bill objected.

'Free,' enticed Georgina, 'gratis. Not a single cent.'

'Where's the catch?'

'No catch.'

'Then——?' He looked suspicious.

'Simple. You tucker me.'

'Tucker you!' Bill looked at her indignantly. 'It's more than the caravan's worth. I'm winding up, Georgina, you know that. What do I want with a van?'

'A van at the price of a ration of flour, sugar, bacon and bully beef!'

'*And* the rest,' groaned Bill. 'I know women.'

'Only I won't be one.'

'What?'

'Only I'll accept whatever you give me,' Georgina changed it adroitly, and Bill gave her a suspicious look, then scratched his head.

'Well, I suppose someone could come along to buy it,' he said dubiously.

Georgina grinned. 'They will. They'll need a caravan and you'll make a handsome profit.'

'I haven't said I'll take it yet.'

'Put in some tinned fruit, too, Bill, some nuts, some——'

'All right, Georgina. When are you pushing off?'

'Tomorrow.'

'Where to? I'll need a forwarding address for your letters.'

She shook her head. 'No letters. I'll write to my friends myself.'

'I don't know if I ought to be in on this; you're a very young girl and it's a very big country.' Bill frowned. 'You're not going to that bloke who sent you the telegram, are you? What was in the telegram, Georgina?'

'No, I suppose when it comes to it I'm not going there.' For the more Georgina thought about it, thought *sanely*, she knew she couldn't go. Masquerading as a man was magazine stuff, it read well, but it couldn't happen. There were too many traps. She thought ruefully that even when she applied for the job she had known in her heart it couldn't happen; that things like that simply didn't come off. But the very act of applying, even of thinking about it, had been stimulating when she needed stimulation ... and from it sprang another idea. She would make for the Lucy River, and on the way she would strike something. It would be very unusual if none of the homesteads she stopped at did not make an offer of a job; they invariably did. Then if they didn't, she could still go on to the Lucy, to Roper's, and remain there, until just before the big boss got back—he had said he would be a few weeks yet—then get out.

'Wherever you're going,' grumbled Bill, 'you seem pleased about it.'

'You should be, too, gaining a free caravan. Make it a beautiful tucker bag, Bill. I'll call tomorrow morning.'

Leaving Windmill Junction might have torn at Georgina if she had been returning to Sydney, but hitting further west instead only lifted her spirits. She waved to everyone she passed as she went into town the next morning to collect her tucker bag, then when she reached the store she rewarded Bill with a kiss.

'So long, old-timer,' she said, 'if you haven't tuckered me well, I'll haunt you.'

Bill scowled. 'Just watch your step, young Georgina, the west isn't what it used to be.'

That was true. These days people did not camp at night just where they found themselves, as in the old days; they sought shelter, and they locked up.

Georgina nodded back at Bill. Travelling in her casual outfit, she had no intention of camping. She would put up each night at a station, a usual thing out here. Homestead wives were always eager for female company.

'Got your survival kit?' Bill grumbled.

'Yes, also essential repair tools and a first aid box,' she confirmed.

'Don't take a wrong road—it's easy out there, wind blows the sand so you can see a dozen roads.'

19

Georgina sighed. 'Bill, I've travelled the desert much more than you have. You've been stuck at your trading post.'

'Emporium,' corrected Bill proudly. 'All right, young Georgina, good luck.' He stood back as she righted her yellow helmet, then kicked the bike into life. 'Should have been a boy,' he grumbled.

'But I am, I'm George.'

Fortunately the cycle drowned that, for Georgina had not intended to say it, it had just burst out. Of course she would never go through with such a harebrained idea. No, she would make for Westleigh tonight, three hundred and fifty kilometres north-west. She and her stepfather had stopped once at Westleigh when Georgina had taken the old man out after a particular rock, and the people at Westleigh had been very welcoming, and most insistent that they come again. Probably they would even find a job for her, superintending the children's correspondence lessons, or doing letters for the station. Georgina avoided a large rut.

Soon the track became as straight as a gun barrel, and strange names began cropping up, names of towns though there were no towns, only a solitary windmill, sometimes not even that. Wombo, Pudda Pudda, Starshine, Smelly Swamp, Begin Again.

Apart from detours for salt pans, clay pans, sticky patches, gibber patches, it was an uneventful morning, but for Georgina a very wonderful one. Joanne might see all this as godforsaken, as the ends of the earth, but Georgina only saw the bare-boned beauty of it, beauty that made mere meadow prettiness fade in comparison.

She passed a few bigger concerns, clusters of chalets, a plastic-lined tank for swimming and a cookhouse wearing a ribbon of smoke. At one, she paused for lunch. These larger outfits comprised project-employed men who did not feel sufficiently personally or financially involved to suspect strangers, and here you were welcome to stop. This bunch told Georgina they were wolfram and mica men, but they were, they grinned, not averse to discovering nickel.

'Or gold?' Georgina grinned back.

During the afternoon she saw a spy plane, a big silver bird in the heraldic blue sky. It certainly would be a spy plane, she knew that from experience, and she stopped the motorcycle to watch the craft dart under a single white cloud. Not a very nice way to make your living, Georgina thought, checking up like that on what a camp was doing, and more important where it was doing it, then selling the information; but that was mining business these days.

She watched the plane return, circle, catch a ray of blazing sun and change into shining gold. The burnished bird against the Bible-blue sky almost hit at her. She stood there and watched and watched and watched . . .

And the harm was done.

No harm, really, except for the fact that she was now much later than she had planned. Georgina checked her watch, checked her map, then realised she really would have to stick at it to make Westleigh by dusk.

At once, almost as though it knew her intention and decided to be spiteful, the track worsened considerably. It narrowed, it bent, it strayed and it rutted. Time after time Georgina had to get off the cycle to manoeuvre the machine over a bad patch. Twice she had to remove her bag, the typewriter and Bill's tucker to make a lighter load . . . what in heaven had Bill put in the tucker bag, it was as heavy as lead . . . and that made, along with the reloading, for more delay.

When she looked at her watch again, she was shocked.

Well, there was nothing for it but to keep going, and at least the road was getting better again.

There were no prospectors now, she was too far out in the country, and that was why Georgina was rather surprised to see the car. Of course cars came, otherwise there would be no call for a road, but she had not expected one this late.

The car was just ahead of her. Ordinarily Georgina would

21

have tooted, stopped and had a friendly word, but now she took the opportunity of a temporary widening of the sandy track to push past. Suddenly she was thinking of Bill's: 'Just watch your step, Georgina, the west isn't what it used to be.'

Once in front of the car, she accelerated and gave the car her dust. She was sorry about that, it was disgusting driving in dust, but it was getting late, and if she was to reach Westleigh ...

To her annoyance, though she kept up her speed, she couldn't shake off the car. It must have been appalling steering into the cloud she had created, and you would have thought the driver would have had more sense and slackened speed, but he still kept up.

Not only did he keep up, he accelerated and then hooted at her and the sound, punctuating the noise of their respective vehicles, alarmed Georgina. What in heaven, she thought, is he doing?

She could not see him clearly in the mirror, all she could see was dust and a vehicle with a figure in the middle of that dust. Perhaps he was harmless ... not perhaps, most certainly he was harmless. Perhaps all he wanted was to be in front, for after all no car driver wants to be beaten by a secondhand sidecar. In which case, decided Georgina, even though it would delay her further he could take the lead. She veered to one side, and after a few moments he passed.

She let him go well ahead and allowed the cloud of dust to disperse. She was impatient to be off, but it seemed a wiser move.

At last she got started again, only to round a stand of bluebush a moment after and see him within distance once more. What was wrong with him? Why was he positively dawdling ... no, actually stopping! ... like this?

For the first time Georgina knew a faint fear. Before she had been aware of danger yet had not really believed in it. It was sensible to take precautions, but one did not really believe anything could happen.

She sized up the situation quickly. The car had not left her any room to pass this time, meaning that she either had to catch up and then stop and confront him, or else turn back, something she could not possibly do at this time of the afternoon. Then—and a delighted giggle escaped her—Georgina saw the second track. What luck! Of all the fortunate places for the fellow to wait this must be the most fortunate one—for her. For undoubtedly it was the only one in miles that offered an alternative route. Evidently the man had not noticed the junction, but Georgina did, and she prepared to veer off to the left. She knew these western tracks very well, how often one road could break up into four or five small roads, then they merged into the one road again. Thank you, mister, Georgina smiled, for stopping where you did and not looking round.

She pushed to the left, very rapidly, so rapidly she only heard him call to her very faintly, so faintly that she decided to consider it no call at all. That will teach him to play city tricks out west, she thought. She kept up her speed, for possibly the track was no short cut, and when the roads met up again she intended to be well ahead of the car, and keep ahead this time.

She kept bouncing along, looking back occasionally for a distant blur of dust, for it was quite likely he would follow her; if not for ulterior motives, then certainly in the belief that she knew a better way. His car, she recalled, was a fast modern one, so it should be appearing by this time. But perhaps he was forging ahead on the other road and would be waiting when the two tracks merged. For a few moments Georgina extended the motorcycle to its utmost. Or perhaps ... she frowned ... he had had no ulterior motive, no anything, and had simply stopped and called out because he had broken down.

Well, that was his bad luck. She tried to say it blithely but did not quite succeed. He could be a newchum out

23

here and not well equipped. Serves him right and all that, but——

But——

'Oh, damn!' Georgina said, turned the cycle and went back.

It was late afternoon now. In the way it did up here, night could surprise you at any minute. There were no preliminaries in these latitudes, night simply fell, then that was that.

Oh, where was that wretched man?

She was back at the junction now and there was no car. More fool her to have returned.

However, even if she had kept going she still would not have made Westleigh, she realised, and annoyed at her bad start on her very first day, Georgina decided to look around for a likely spot to spend the night. At least a cycle, even one with a sidecar, could be put in a more concealed position—no, she wouldn't say concealed, she would say sheltered—than a car could; and Georgina chose a thicket of mulga and pushed the cycle into the middle of it.

She decided to eat while it was still light, so she took out the hamper and rugs while she could still see them, got into the sidecar and made herself snug. When night came it would be pitch dark for an hour and impossible to find anything. After that it would be dark blue and deep gold and very lovely ... if one had the nerve to watch it. She smiled.

But she watched safely now as she ate, watched a wedge-tailed eagle rise high in a sky of fast-deepening bluebell, watched a spotted harrier looking down for his prey. What if he mistook her for a goody? No, he was pouncing on another poor victim. Georgina shut her eyes from the sight of it ... and that started it, started a sleep that as far as she was concerned went on too long. She had not intended to sleep, she had intended to watch; but sleep she did, and the noise that awakened her was not the beat of the harrier's wings, the struggle of the unhappy prey, it was a man's footsteps.

There was a car there, too. The same car she had passed and given her dust, then afterwards allowed to pass her. Wherever he had been, she didn't know, and evidently he did not know where she had been either, for he called out:

'What are you playing at? Is it some kind of game?'

Then he came across.

'Just watch your step, Georgina,' Bill had said, and Georgina had agreed that things weren't the same any more and resolved she would do just that.

But who wanted things the same with a man like this, a man smiling warmly at you, putting out his hand to you, a man with a flick of sunbleached hair, bright hazel eyes and a friendly smile?

Georgina smiled back and put her own hand out to his.

'I'm sorry——' she began.

'No, *I* am. I can see it all very clearly now. You thought that I——'

'Yes?' Georgina asked.

'That I might be a menace?'

'Well, yes, I'm afraid I did,' she admitted.

'It wasn't that at all.'

'I hope not.'

He grinned and said: 'I was simply trying to attract your attention not to take the turn-off. It comes to a dead end.'

'But it didn't,' she protested.

'Then you can't have gone far enough to find out. Why did you come back?'

'I ... well, I got worried about you.'

'*Touché.*' He smiled again. 'I did the same.'

Georgina met his smile with hers once more.

'Seems we've been two idiots,' the man said. 'Where were you heading?'

'Westleigh.'

'You wouldn't have made it, anyway. Not by dark.'

25

'No,' Georgina agreed. She asked: 'And you?'

He shrugged. 'I do this trip fairly frequently and I couldn't inflict myself on a station every time, so I've converted the car for sleeping. You'll find it comfortable.'

'Oh no, I won't.'

He grinned all the way at that, but he didn't argue.

'Please yourself, then. How are you for rations?'

'I've eaten.'

'Wise girl, it'll be dark in five minutes.'

'And bright again in an hour,' she pointed out.

'Then you know the Inside?'

'Yes.'

'A pity you won't accept some creature comfort,' he shrugged, 'we could swap stories. There's nothing like Inside stories.'

'I know,' Georgina agreed a little wistfully, 'but there's also nothing like country convention.' She said it very properly, even though a smile was not far away.

He saw the smile and played along. 'So long as it's just convention stopping you and not fear.'

'It's what I said,' she assured with a quirk. 'Goodnight.'

'Goodnight,' he saluted.

Georgina rearranged her cushions and rugs, and by that time it was dark. Instant Night, she and her stepfather had called it. She lay back and looked up.

The bush had never disturbed her. She was, she supposed, no child of Pan; it was the children of Pan who saw and heard and imagined things. The silence and emptiness of remote places had never brought that choking panic that it did to some people, to Pan's people. I'm just a natural for the outback, Georgina congratulated herself, I'm khaki-coloured, ordinary and tough.

I'm George, in short ... or I would be if I could go through with it. But it's too ridiculous, and I won't.

She watched the darkness until at last the stars broke through, big blossoms of stars and a moon the size of a melon. Occasional movements of small animals, perhaps

26

reptiles, did not disturb her. When a dingo howled a long way off, she chided: 'Lie down, yellow dog!'

She wondered idly and rather pleasantly about that nice man in the car. A writer looking for material? A pastoralist returning home? Obviously he wasn't a stockman, nor a drover or horse-breaker, he didn't wear the right clothes. He could be a geologist, she supposed. She wondered where he was going.

She started eliminating different places, and then, in spite of her previous sleep, she became drowsy doing it.

A small noise aroused her. It could have been a kangaroo, a yellow dog, and yet it seemed somehow a human noise, like footsteps. Feet made a different sound from paws or hooves.

There it went again, a stir. A slither. A step.

Then suddenly there was a scatter of something on the windscreen in front of her ... she did not know what it was, nor wait to find out, she simply leapt from the cycle outfit and fled to the car, calling as she went. Except that Georgina was shaking with fright and not focusing properly, she would have noticed that the man was already out of his car and waiting with the door open for her to get in.

But she didn't notice.

She said breathlessly: 'I thought ... I woke up ... there was this sound ...'

He said soothingly: 'Get in.'

Georgina did.

They talked for hours. He had much to tell her about the north-west, and that was what Georgina wanted. Tentatively during the conversation she brought in the Lucy River, Big Lucy, and his descriptions thrilled her. Yes, it was beautiful, he said, in the big river country. There was colour to spare, he related, flowers everywhere now, not coastal flowers but flowers without a name; flood flowers you could call them perhaps, scarlet, magenta, orange, gold, and always, of course, the Salvation Jane.

Waterbirds had arrived, he told her. It was common to

27

see ibis, swans and pelicans, but most remarkable of all were the gulls. All those hundreds of miles from the coast, there were gulls.

But when Georgina asked, casually she hoped, about Roper's, the man became oddly reticent. Odd, that was, for the outgoing type he obviously was. But Georgina believed she understood. That fellow Roper, she thought, in spite of his confirming and quite friendly telegram, had sounded the pig of pigs.

Around midnight Georgina slept, and carefully the man beside her removed some telltale gravel that had fallen to the floor of the car. He had gathered the gravel and stored it, then waited for the opportunity to throw it at the side-car's windscreen, and the ruse had worked. He grinned as he placed another rug over Georgina, a pillow under her head.

Then he regarded her for quite a while. It was a very close, very experienced look.

At last he shrugged, smiled philosophically, and then he, too, slept.

CHAPTER THREE

Georgina woke to the sound of music and the smell of coffee.

'Both canned,' her companion called from outside the car, 'I'm no pioneer.' He nodded to the battery transistor and a small spirit stove. 'Did you sleep well?'

'Wonderfully. I didn't hear you lower the seat.'

'You were drifting off by that time, so I did it very carefully. Aren't you glad now you didn't sleep in the sidecar? You could have had a shockingly stiff neck.'

'Yes, I'm glad,' admitted Georgina, 'I was pleased to go anywhere last night. I was sure I heard steps, then something was thrown across the windscreen. It sounded like gravel or small pebbles. Ah!' Georgina sat up and looked with deep intrigue at some fine stones on the floor of the car that the man had evidently missed.

'*You* threw it,' she accused.

'I plead guilty. I couldn't have you sitting out there, yet I know how stubborn women are.'

She looked at him in disbelief, yet a disbelief with a smile not far behind. 'Is that the truth, or did you really have ulterior motives?' she demanded. He was a very easy person to talk to, Georgina found.

'I had ulterior motives.' The man pretended to hang his head. 'Only——'

'Only?'

'Only you looked like my kid sister if I'd had one,' he grinned.

'Sure it wasn't your brother?' Georgina touched her short-cropped head.

29

'Now I didn't like to say that,' he laughed.

'I don't mind. Well, I'd better not mind seeing that I——'

'Yes?'

'I'm not stubborn.' Georgina returned to safe ground.

'All females are.'

'You sound rather like Roper of Lucy River when you talk like that.' Georgina had not intended to bring up Roper again after her companion's previous reticence, and she bit her lip.

But she needn't have worried. The man looked across at her and asked:

'So you know him?'

She shook her head. 'No.'

'Yet you just said——'

'Let's put it that I've gathered an impression of him.'

'Such as?'

'As if he's the way you just sounded when you called me stubborn.'

'And that adds up to?'

'A disliker of females,' she asserted, 'no, not a disliker in your case, for your "stubborn" was only in fun, wasn't it?'

'It was.' He was watching her intently.

'But anything from him would come from a born woman-hater, I think.'

'Not born, achieved. But yes, you've got it right.'

Georgina's companion had made himself a cup of coffee and he got in behind the wheel to drink it beside her.

'In all our talk last night we never got round to names,' he told her. 'I'm Craig Everson.'

'Georgina Brown,' she told him.

'I was born up here, and, apart from school, reared up here. Then when my father died I inherited the station.' A shrug. 'Small and badly run down. It wasn't the old man's fault, it was the drop in beef prices. He, then I, had the bad luck to coincide with the first cattle slump in years. The failure didn't worry me, I was never keen, but the lack of funds did. Eventually I had to lease the place out and take

30

on this travelling job. Interested in any farm machinery, Miss Brown?'

'No,' Georgina smiled. 'So even though you were born pioneer stock, the real instinct isn't there?'

'Not at all. I do this job only because I know it, know the country, know the people. If I knew the city as well, you'd never see me past the coast.'

'And yet you spoke so graphically about it last night.'

'Of course. I love it, but only to look at and then go away again. I'm not a Larry Roper.'

'Does he love it?'

'Blindly,' Craig grinned.

'Is that his name, Larry?'

'I thought you'd know.'

'No, I don't know,' Georgina confessed.

There was silence for a while. Craig Everson had produced breakfast biscuits and adroitly covered them with portions of canned bacon.

'Lovely,' Georgina appreciated.

'Better than you would have served yourself?'

'Oh yes, but I do have supplies, I'm well tuckered.'

'You sound as though you're really going somewhere. Somewhere further, I'd say, than the Westleigh you told me last night.' His gaze was keen.

'Yes, I am going further now. Westleigh would have been only an overnight stay.'

'Will you call in regardless?'

'I think not,' she said.

'Then where?'

'You do want to know a lot, don't you?' Georgina laughed.

'I do,' Craig admitted. 'I like company, particularly female company. To be truthful, in spite of my brotherly feelings for you last night, I have the reputation up here of something of a womaniser.'

'Deserved?' she asked mischievously.

He grinned, shrugged and didn't answer that. 'Also,' he

went on, 'although I can wax lyrical about it, I really dislike the bush. I guess I'm just a city slicker at heart. I like to be hemmed in, both with people and chatter.'

'Then I'll chatter,' promised Georgina.

He was easy to talk to and easy to get on with, and when, their coffee and breakfast biscuits finished, Craig suggested that they travelled within hailing distance of each other, Georgina was happy to agree.

It was reassuring to have a man in sight, she thought as she bounced along behind Craig Everson, near enough to see him but sufficiently far away to escape his dust.

She was doubly sure of this when the motorcycle began playing up some time later, then finally stopped. Within minutes Craig was back by her side again, but it took him an hour to spark the reluctant engine.

'Where did you get it?' he despaired. 'In a lucky dip? If so, I can assure you that you weren't lucky.'

'We gave very little for it,' Georgina admitted.

'We?'

'My stepfather and I. For the small outlay we've had good service.'

'Well, I can tell you one thing, it won't be serving you much longer,' Craig said.

'But it has to! I have to get there.'

'Where?' he demanded.

'I—I'm not sure. I mean I was, and then—— Well, I had second thoughts. Oh, dear, I'm not making any sense.'

'More sense than you think,' he said shrewdly. 'It's to do with the Lucy, isn't it? You've been pumping me hard enough.'

'Well——'

'And to do with Larry Roper?'

'How would you know that?'

'How would I know, the lady asks, after oh-so-carefully yet oh-so-obviously cross-examining me from the moment we met!' Craig laughed aloud.

'I'm sure I didn't.'

'Well, how do you explain now that I'm right about Lucy and Roper?' He grinned at her.

'You're not right. I'm going to the first station that can find a niche for me. Any project that needs a cook or a clerk or a——'

'But that wasn't the original intention.'

'Yes ... no.'

He ignored that. 'Roper's was?'

'Well—yes,' she admitted.

'Did I change your mind, saying the things I did about him?' he inquired solicitously.

'No, I think I changed my mind myself, and before you spoke.'

'Why?'

'Because,' Georgina admitted with a grin, for she found Craig Everson extraordinarily easy to talk to, 'a girl can't be a man.' She gave him a triumphant look. 'Now I've got you,' she challenged.

He laughed. 'You haven't really! I believe I can see it all. You've answered an ad from Roper asking for a man.'

'Did you read it?'

'No, but I know you wouldn't be going out there unless you had something in view, and I also know that Roper would never advertise for a woman, not now. So this time,' Craig Everson grinned, 'I've got *you*.'

'Well, yes, I did do just that,' she admitted, 'I did answer an advertisement for a man. It seemed all right then, but afterwards I knew I was being crazy.'

'Very true; very crazy, and it wouldn't work. Roper's an eagle, nothing escapes him. But then it probably wouldn't work if you were the other sex—not many men can put up with the Mighty Roper.'

'Mighty Roper?'

'He's called that out here.'

'Because he's mighty?'

'Because he thinks he is,' he amended.

'You don't like him,' guessed Georgina.

33

'No.'

'Any reason?'

'Plenty. My main one is that he messed up my life.'

Georgina looked at Craig curiously, and decided he didn't appear to have a messed-up life. She felt he had more to say, and being Craig would certainly say it, so she waited.

'His own life had been messed around,' Craig obliged, 'but that was no reason why mine should be, too.'

'A girl?' asked Georgina shrewdly.

'Yes. She was Roper's fiancée. Like most hard, tough westerners Larry Roper fell hard and tough for Elva. He put everything into his plans for her.'

'And?'

'Well, she got bored with his plans and tore them up. Not literally, of course, but she let Roper know that for her he was only a diversion.'

'Then where did you come in?'

'Elva had become interested in me, just as I was interested in her.'

'Then why didn't you ... Oh, I'm sorry, it was the money, I suppose, I mean the lack of it,' she said, confused.

'No, it was him.' Craig sounded terse.

'Him?'

'Roper, of course. He bought her off. Larry Roper gave Elva the money to clear out. Not just to Sydney but overseas—big money she couldn't resist.'

'Go on,' she urged. He shrugged.

'Need I? Can't you understand that it was a case of "if I can't have her neither can you" as applied to me?'

'He could have been considering you, thinking you shouldn't be hurt as well,' Georgina suggested, though unconvinced herself.

'Only it wasn't; it was pure Roper. He's like that. Look, Georgina, for your own good put any ideas out of your mind as regards going to this man. Not only is he soured by women, he's a tyrant to his own sex. You couldn't win either way. If you went as a female he would show you the way out, and if you went as a male——'

'He'd kick me out?'

'I think,' said Craig, 'you have the general idea.'

'Yet he did advertise,' Georgina demurred.

'Forget it.'

'And do what instead?' she asked.

'I wish I could offer you something, only I'm barely able to keep going myself.' Craig gave a rueful shrug. 'I wouldn't put much reliance on landing a job at any of the stations, either. The boom has been remarkable for its non-appearance this year, and the stations simply aren't putting on extra hands.'

'Well, I'm still not going back,' Georgina said with all the stubbornness of which he had previously accused her, 'this is my kind of country. Here I belong.'

'Famous last words!' he mocked.

'I mean them.'

'Then it's on your shoulders.' He looked slyly at Georgina. 'Incidentally,' he probed, 'a girl's shoulders or a boy's?'

'I told you that I'd finished with that idea,' she told him.

'Yes, but I think you could change your mind.'

'Then which do you advise?'

'Which?' he echoed blankly.

'Male or female shoulders?'

'Neither.'

'But if you *were* advising,' she persisted.

'Determined baggage, aren't you?' he grinned at her.

'Which?' she insisted.

'I'd say a male's shoulders. A woman wouldn't last two minutes there.'

Georgina was thoughtful. 'Yet he must have loved her,' she said at length.

'Elva?'

'Yes. I mean, you said it was a lot of money that he gave her.'

'He has a lot,' Craig said drily.

35

By mutual unspoken consent they dropped the subject. Georgina climbed on to the motorcycle again and began following the car as she had before.

Later in the afternoon the old machine gave up altogether. Craig spent another hour on it, then turned and advised Georgina to kiss it goodbye.

'But what will I do? How will I get there?'

'Get where?' he asked once more, and this time Georgina didn't evade the question.

'Roper's,' she said.

'So you are going?' His eyes narrowed.

'Yes.'

'I suppose I should say find your own way, then, and that anyone who goes to him deserves what she gets.'

'No, *he* gets,' corrected Georgina.

'You mean——'

'Yes, I mean that, Craig. There's simply nothing else for me to do. You said yourself there would be no jobs being offered, and I can't, and I won't, go back. I'm going as George Brown. *He* thinks I'm George Brown, so I'm that far at least, and he, Roper, won't be back for a few weeks yet, so I could stay on until the eleventh hour, as it were.'

'But if he did come before——' Craig began.

'He won't. He said so.'

'But——'

'Then I'd still be all right. The cabin, my cabin, is secluded, there's no one close. Finally, if he did discover me' ... a little rueful grin ... 'you must agree I'm no *femme fatale.*'

'It's a matter of opinion,' Craig said gallantly.

'Thank you. But you still must agree that I—well——'

'I believe that you're trying to say, among other things, that you have a boyish figure,' he laughed.

'Flat,' she agreed.

'Not in all places ... hi, I didn't deserve that!' She had thrown a handful of pebbles at him.

'You did. But please continue being frank.'

36

Craig studied her. 'Then I believe you could pass muster —male muster. Your hair's a bit short, though, for males these days.'

'*He* should approve of that,' she said with spirit.

'Well, I'm not approving, Georgina, in fact I'm dead against it all. It's a fool thing to do.'

'Any alternative?' she asked him.

'No, but you'll never get away with it. The man, as I said, is an eagle, and he'd get you in the end. And being the eagle he is, that end will be right at the beginning.'

Georgina sighed. 'Well, at least I'll have it all over, Craig, but I'm still certain. I'm George Brown, and I'm going to Roper's in answer to an ad. If you're around to pick up the pieces when I'm kicked out, I'll be grateful, but if you're not, I guess I'll still survive.'

Craig also sighed, but he did not argue. 'You'll know where to come when you're kicked out?'

'Everson's?' she queried.

'Bryden's now; I've leased the place, remember, but they'll put you up until I come on my next round, and then I can give you a lift home.'

'The old motorcycle here is home,' she responded wryly.

'Yes, I think you made that clear, too clear. Now, shall we bury the body?'

The old cycle was stripped of everything that could be used, then they left it there. An hour later with Georgina reclining much more comfortably in the car than in the sidecar, they made camp for the night once more.

'You're nice, Craig,' Georgina said that evening as they watched the stars come out.

'I think you actually mean I'm safe,' he grinned.

'Perhaps. Is it because of Elva? Or' ... slyly ... 'is it because I'm so obviously a George?'

He grinned again and they relapsed into a comfortable silence that deepened into sleep.

The next morning they set off at daybreak. They wanted to

make journey's end by the afternoon.

Craig was frankly worried about delivering Georgina, and he told her so, relating how he had been ordered off the place. 'We had,' he said in obvious understatement, 'a few pertinent words.'

'About Elva?' she asked.

'Yes.'

'He sounds the lord of all creation, impossible, vainglorious,' she said, thinking of the cattle boss.

'Mighty Roper is. He's arrogance itself.'

'I see. Well, you can put me off at the gate.'

'And make you walk five kilometres with all your gear?'

'Is it that far?' She was taken aback.

'At least,' he agreed.

'It should be safe enough to take me,' Georgina said thoughtfully, 'the telegram said he wouldn't be back for several weeks.'

'Then we'll give it a go. Georgina, you *are* sure?'

'Sure,' she nodded.

'If only I could offer you an alternative. Even—well—offer myself.' He was frowning thoughtfully.

'Yourself?'

'As an employer ... or even as a partner if it was a way out.'

'Partner?' she asked suspiciously.

'Husband,' he grinned.

'But you're not offering, are you?'

'No,' Craig agreed apologetically, 'I'm not.'

They did not speak much for the rest of the journey. Georgina for her part was tense and excited and she could see that Craig was uneasy. What kind of man was this Roper, she seethed, to make everyone wretched like this? Just because a girl hadn't fallen into his arms——

She asked Craig about that, and he said: 'I think it was the first time that Mighty Roper had ever been thwarted. Everything had always come easy to him, everything had fallen into his lap. The station ... a big thriving concern, not like my poor holding ... had escaped any down trend through its sheer size. Also, the minerals Roper has dug up have all been sound. I really believe Larry's failure with Elva was his only failure in a singularly successful life.'

'And he couldn't take it?'

'Exactly,' Craig said.

'Then he wants a lesson,' Georgina vowed. He stared.

'You're not thinking of playing teacher, are you?'

'I'm only a student, didn't I tell you? I'm doing a thesis while I work.'

'You're really serious over all this, aren't you?'

'Yes, Craig.' She looked determined. 'It's going to be all right, it has to be—well, for a while at least.'

'Then just watch what you're doing, that's all.'

Craig had taken his eyes off the road a moment to emphasize his words, and the eyes suddenly met Georgina's for the first time. He looked much longer than he should, and when he turned his gaze back to the track again he was quiet, bemused.

Georgina made several attempts to break the silence, then she became quiet as well.

In the mid-afternoon Georgina made Craig pull up while she attended to a few adjustments; the adjustments comprised slicking back her short hair, rubbing off any vestige of lipstick, and loosening her shirt and wearing it outside of her pants instead of tucked in, fortunately an accepted way in the west to defeat the heat. It also succeeded in taking away any shape from her, which, being over-slim, she didn't have anyhow, she grimaced.

'Do I look sufficiently male?' she asked the man at last.

'You look——' he stopped.

'Yes?'

'You look—beautiful.'

'Oh, stop playing the fool, Craig,' Georgina said irritably, and got back into the car.

Some time later he turned into a gate and started down a long peppercorn-bordered drive. Around the five-kilometre mark a large homestead loomed up; wide verandahs, dozens of rooms, the usual country abode.

Craig nodded to a big front door. 'You'd better inquire,' he told Georgina.

'I will. Just keep your fingers crossed.'

Georgina crossed to the entrance, a double portal flung wide, and knocked. A middle-aged woman came down a long hall, exchanged friendly words, then handed Georgina a key.

'It's half a mile down the valley,' she directed. Georgina could see no valley, but she knew how country people can find a hill in a small mound, so she understood. 'You'll find it well stocked. Anything else you want, come back here.'

'I'm afraid I can't. My motorcycle gave up and I was brought here.' Georgina had always despaired of her deep, rather husky tone, but now it was a blessing.

'Once you get there you'll be all right, son. George, isn't it? I think Mr Roper said that.'

'George. George Brown,' she muttered.

'I'm Mrs Willmott, but they all call me Willy. Mr Roper left his motorcycle at the cabin for you, George; if your friend took you down, you could find your own way after that on the bike.'

'Thank you. When are you expecting Mr Roper?'

'Not for a few weeks yet. Don't forget, if there's anything you need——' The woman was turning back. Evidently she was cooking, or doing something that needed her attention, for she did not even glance at Craig.

Georgina went back to the car, swinging the key triumphantly.

'First hurdle over,' she gloated.

'Meaning nothing.' Craig did not gloat with her. 'Georgina——' he began.

'George. Even she said so.' Georgina was bubbling over.

'Georgina, I've been thinking it over.'

'Drive down, please,' she requested.

'But, Georgina——'

'George, Craig, and please drive on.'

They passed paddocks, empty paddocks, resting paddocks, and paddocks with stock obviously awaiting transport to the abattoirs.

'Poor things,' sighed Georgina.

'Men don't talk like that,' Craig reminded her.

'Do I have to be a man with you?'

'No.' Now Craig was looking fully at her, and the look lasted so long this time that the car wandered and Georgina had to lean over to right the wheel.

'For heaven's sake, Craig!' she said.

'Yes, I suppose so. Well, here's your hut now. Got your key?' He extended his hand to open the door for her, but Georgina was already out of reach. She felt she had had enough for today, and somehow Craig wasn't being such a help any more.

'Thanks, Craig,' she called, 'I'll never forget your kindness. Just throw my gear out. Then you'd better get going.'

'Georgina, I——'

'Get going, Craig.'

'I'll carry your bags in at least,' he protested.

'No. No! I'm a man. I'm a feller.'—Joanne's tag.—'What if anyone sees?'

'But you will get in touch?' he appealed.

'I will,' she promised.

Before he could start again, Georgina grabbed up an armful of luggage and fairly raced with it to the hut door. She had to put everything down to open up, but she did it so quickly and so adroitly that he had no chance at all of following her, of beginning another conversation. He had been helpful, he had been sweet really, and she couldn't have done without him, but——

She fairly threw the things in, then she went in after them, slammed the door and turned the key. She would collect the remaining luggage after he had left.

It was some time before he went, she thought. What on earth was keeping him? He had been anxious not to come here before, he had said he had been warned off the place, yet now he didn't seem to want to go.

Men, Georgina thought in despair, men!

'Yet I,' Georgina looked around her and found a speckled mirror tacked to the wall and went across to it to address a khaki-haired boy who looked back at her, 'am about to become one myself.'

CHAPTER FOUR

Yes, Georgina decided, she was going to be a man. For several weeks (less a day to enable her to get away in time) she was going to hide here and decide what she wanted next out of life. No, that was wrong, she *knew* what she wanted; she wanted the inland, but she knew, too, she couldn't have it. So she was going to hide out and ponder on the next best.

Meanwhile she was going to revel in it all, drown herself in the gold of it, sink herself in the Mirage Country that she loved so much. Possibly . . . no, more likely, and it was a sad thought . . . it would be for the last time. Once she went back to the city there would be nothing to bring her here again. So while she could she would take the bike out, find a track and ride and ride into the distance, and somewhere during the ride a mirage would appear—the blue swimming scene to which her stepfather had given a scientific explanation yet a romantic one as well. A thing of dreams to Georgina.

'Perfect,' she said aloud, coming back to the present, and she began looking around her.

The hut was small but comprehensive, a stark hut for a male occupant. A plain wooden bed with a plain cover, brown table, brown dresser, hooks on the walls to hang clothes. She must remember to hang only male-type clothing.

There was sufficient cooking gear but certainly nothing fancy, and, characteristic of a man, it was placed within easy reach. Simple saucepans, a frying pan, a kettle. Cutlery but no tablecloth on which to place it, just the bare table.

43

There was a rag rug on the floor and a flypaper curl from the ceiling, and that was all.

Where did she shower or bath? Lots of such places had portable arrangements, or squares enclosed modestly in hessian attached to an outside wall. Georgina looked but found nothing—oh, yes, there *was* something—a large uncovered shower rose extended from the tank. She shrank back. If Mr Larry Roper thought she was going to bathe out there without concealment he had another thought coming. Why, even men prefer not to go on display!

She toyed with the idea of adapting the bedcover for privacy. Even though the hut was isolated, a long way from the activities of the homestead and ninety-nine per cent obscure, she still did not fancy standing outside every morning to soap and scrub. Yet such a method as a draped bedcover would only soak the cover, and by the heavy texture of the coarse cretonne it would take a long while to dry.

Eventually she unearthed a large plastic basin. Evidently the previous males had done their washing in this, for some faded daubs of laundry blue still remained. Well, shrugged Georgina, she had bathed in a basin before.

One thing that did please her was the size of the table. She could spread out Stepfather's papers at one end, yet still find room to eat or read at the other end. Mr Roper had been fair at least when he mentioned the advantages for a student. He had said he allowed free time, and undoubtedly he had supplied a table that really invited industriousness. Georgina took all her papers out of her bag first and left the other items for later.

Before her stepfather died, he and Georgina had spoken eagerly about presenting his data in a more acceptable form to the layman as a change from the usual learned and heavy discourses; Stepfather was to provide Georgina with the facts and Georgina to write them in a more animated style than was currently adopted, a style to catch the people who take up a book in interest then have to put it down to complete some task. The first chapters had turned out well and received Sepfather's approval. If only she could keep it up ...

She stacked the work neatly—bachelors were noted to be neat, even pernickety, she reminded herself. Perhaps I'm not a bachelor, perhaps I'm married, even a young father, she thought frantically, after all, the only stipulation was that she should be male.

Next she inspected the supplies from the station. There were potatoes, onions, flour, sugar, tea, coffee, and a selection of tinned goods. The small kerosene fridge would be a boon in this weather, she appreciated, and as she didn't fancy lighting up a range every day, because that would mean collecting, then chopping wood, plus a hot room afterwards, she was glad there was a kerosene variety of stove as well.

The fridge when she opened it held a wedge of corned brisket and a supply of beer; men's viands. But when, later, she opened Bill's tucker to put away any perishables, she found both cordial and sherry, so everything balanced out nicely.

To celebrate the moment, the first moment, she opened the sherry.

She sat on the doorstep of the hut and sipped slowly. Stepfather always had said that no one had seen a sunset until they had seen one here in the interior; it was getting towards dusk now, so Georgina watched. At Windmill Junction life had been slow, taking no count of hours, especially at the darkling hour, but here there seemed a complete standstill as though time itself had ceased to exist. Even the heat haze that always danced on these horizons had settled now to a still blue smoke.

Then it happened—all the colour in the world bursting out at the same wonderful moment, brilliant red, deep violet, flaunting pink and splendid gold. She wanted to jump up and embrace it all, to call out her delight, to cheer. Then she remembered in time that men don't do things like that. Yet they appreciated beauty, for her stepfather had, and Larry Roper, Craig had said, 'blindly' loved this place. Perhaps that was what made Roper so difficult; his love was all used up, nothing left over. Well, she'd leave all that for another day, the day after she left here to be exact. Until then she would simply enjoy herself and not think about men and what made them tick, even though she was supposed to be one herself.

She had every intention of being fair to the employer who would never employ her, though, for she intended to do as much exploring as she could and to leave a full report when she went. At least he had got her here, so he deserved that much. Suddenly feeling the stress of travelling for three days, Georgina got up, made herself a sketchy meal from one of the tins and then went to bed.

The bed was comfortable but hard, the kind she believed men preferred, so she must prefer it too. Did Craig sleep at the Brydens' when he was up here? A nice man, Craig, she thought drowsily. A shame about the girl Elva whom the mighty Roper had removed so that Craig, or any man she supposed, couldn't win where he had failed. Odd to think that a place like this could stage its little scandals, too. Craig, Elva, Roper. Larry Roper. Was Larry short for Lawrence? Or was it short for Lucy? She gave a long yawn. Lucy. Big Lucy. The Lucy River.

Georgina slept.

She awoke at dawn to primrose light buttering the uncurtained windowsill. There were no curtains anywhere, and Georgina felt tempted to make some from an old floral dress she hadn't wanted to bring but had, because she had nowhere to leave it. I mustn't, though, she thought sternly, that's woman's stuff. I must remember I'm George.

She bathed in the basin and cooked herself breakfast, then she began exploring outside.

She found the motorcycle and a quantity of petrol beside it, so she kicked the engine over and drove round the hut. The bike drove well and was easy to manage. She felt tempted to go further afield, but she decided to examine her nearer environs first.

She was surprised at the green grass and the variety of flowers, flowers she did not recognise—flood flowers, Craig had called them. They grew more thickly here than any she had seen on the track coming up, but then this terrain must have received more rain, for the property was on the Lucy. Knowing the distances of the west, Georgina would not have liked to guess how far she was from the river. Probably in the Dry, when the river dwindled, it could be as much as a hundred kilometres, but following the Wet, as it was now, as little as several kilometres. That was one of the pleasant discoveries she would put away for later.

But work came first, work for the boss who had made all this possible. Georgina pulled on a canvas hat and began scouting around, firstly on foot.

Even close to the hut the prospect was promising. There were several blackbutt trees, which was often a nickel indication, and some of the rock near them seemed likely host rock. Georgina believed there might even be the end of a serpentine belt. Where did the belt start?

She decided not to look closely now but to look instead at the station. She left the bike where it was and walked the half-mile up to the homestead, hoping that she would encounter no one on the way. She and Craig had seen no one yesterday.

But that, she soon realised, was an impossibility on a cattle station. Yesterday must have been an exception. Men were working in the paddocks, and they all waved to her. One called out: 'How's signs, Geo?' to show he knew the language of her work.

Georgina hoped she made a suitably friendly, non-committal, mannish reply.

She had not meant to call in at the homestead, but the housekeeper was on the verandah and saw her, so there was nothing for it but to go across when the woman went inside, to return holding aloft the time-honoured signal for tea.

They had it together in the big kitchen, and Georgina remembered to sit right according to Tom Sawyer. Knees apart for girls, Mark Twain had written, so that their dresses could catch a ball, but knees together for boys because a boy has no assisting skirt.

Mrs Willmott, meanwhile, was relating to Georgina how she was the only woman on the station.

'What about the wives?' Georgina asked. 'Aren't any of the stockmen married?'

'None. They're all like Mr Roper, bachelors. But don't go getting any ideas that Mr Roper orders it like that, he doesn't. He simply prefers it himself, especially since——' But Mrs Willmott did not finish that.

'No,' she proceeded proudly, 'Mr Roper never dictates. Very tolerant, Mr Roper. He even has parties here at times for the younger ones. There are not many young fellows these days, they all drift to the city. We hold the do's in the big barn. Then'—and Mrs Willmott smiled at Georgina—'I'm not the only woman. You'll enjoy yourself at the parties, George. There are plenty of pretty girls. My goodness, you do have a small appetite, not like my cattle boys.'

'They use up more energy,' Georgina suggested, 'but I'd like to take back a piece of your brownie for supper.'

'You'll take the whole brownie, and some Hard Times.'

'Hard Times?' she queried.

'We call the cookies Hard Times here. And you'll take another loaf of bread,' decreed Mrs Willmott.

'I've barely begun the bread you left.'

'But you must have fresh bread. Shall I send some down each day?'

'No,' said Georgina hurriedly, 'I'll come for it.'

'Yes, I think that's better. You don't want to bury yourself, do you, you want to come up here, otherwise you'll be turning into a rock specimen yourself. But I guess the men will be after you.'

'A-After me?' Georgina faltered.

'To make up a hand of poker.'

'Poker?'

'Or to join a game of snooker. They have regular competitions.'

'Yes,' said Georgina faintly. 'Well, I'd better get back now. You still haven't heard any definite date for Mr Roper?'

'None yet. But he'll fly in when he's ready.'

'Fly?' she queried.

'He always flies. One thing, out here there are plenty of landing strips,' Mrs Willmott laughed.

Georgina left her presently, not knowing whether to feel pleased about the mighty Roper flying back or not. Flying in meant that Mr Roper could return much faster, yet on the other hand it also meant he could not surprise her as he might by car. You could not possibly conceal a plane, not in this great blue inverted bowl of a sky. Also the sound of a craft, even a small one, would cut through the quiet and alert her. I could be packed and out before the mighty Roper touched down, Georgina smiled. But meanwhile she wanted to get some work done.

She spent the afternoon examining, marking and noting any possible findings in her book. When she had finished she wrote it all up in detailed precision.

The rest of the week went like that. As well as 'signs' of nickel she found other minerals, as she had learned from her stepfather. Craig had been right when he had called this mighty Roper mineral-lucky, she decided.

They were enjoyable days. Georgina would explore in the morning, note her finds back at the hut, then put in several hours on the book. These things, and collecting her needs from the homestead, saw to it that time did not hang on her hands.

She had no tricky moments. Once one of the cattlemen came across to the fence to ask her to join them at cards, but when Georgina explained she had work to finish, he nodded sympathetically.

'We might work harder while the work's on,' he grinned, 'but you poor geos work harder when the work's over. Well, boy, you know where to come for a beer and a yarn.'

'Thanks,' Georgina said.

At the end of the week she felt so relaxed she could not think of herself as the same strung-up girl who had faced Joanne in a cramped caravan and said miserably: 'What plans could I have?'

Joanne! Georgina made a little face. She realised she must write down very soon to Joanne, tide her over, beg for a little time and make some satisfactory explanation, otherwise Joanne would want to know what was happening, and, being Joanne, set about finding out.

But nothing *was* happening, and it was wonderful that way. Yet—— Yet—— Georgina knew it could not last, and that actually she did not want it to last, not really. She was no introvert, she liked and she enjoyed company. It was just that Stepfather's passing had left her empty, and that she needed a time like this to recover before she started to fill her life again. Another week the same as this week, and she might even take a risk and accept that invitation for a beer and a yarn, she smiled to herself. No, she could never be a hermit.

She did not accept any invitation, of course, it would have been too hazardous; but she did take long drives into the scrub, mostly looking for the Lucy, which must be more miles away than she had thought, since she never succeeded in reaching it. But she did experience her beloved mirages, which sometimes took the form of dancing blue lakes with little boats set on them, once a shining river with banks and trees. Was it true, as Stepfather had said, that these mirages were actual scenes plucked up by the sky and repeated somewhere else? Was someone at this minute sailing in one of those little boats, someone sitting on a bank under one of those trees?

It was often hard for Georgina to believe that the dancing

50

water she saw was not real but only 'pretend'. Once she even halted the cycle to jump off and run towards the scene to find out. It was quite absurd of her, she knew, but——

But she found water!

Yes, it was real, not fantasy, but it was not a branch of the Lucy, it was an old wurlie. Wurlies were aboriginal waterholes, but this one could not have been used for years, for it was overgrown, yet charmingly overgrown. In every way it was a very pretty spot. Caught up in rocks, almost cradled in them, its base and sides were stone instead of earth so that in place of green algae to take away the water's sparkle it was as brightly clean as if it had been specially built there. The aftermath of the Wet had wreathed it round in vines and flowers, making a perfect setting. Dancing in the sun yet sufficiently shade-dappled to promise coolness, the wurlie was quite irresistible. Georgina looked at it for one moment only, then the next moment she was instinctively peeling off her clothes and splashing into the water. After bathing for a week in a basin she could think of nothing more heavenly.

She dived under, then surfaced. She let the sweet water encompass her, eyes, ears, head, all of her. She felt the short strands of her hair moving with the ripples she made, her body drinking in the gentle coolness.

But she was making no ripples when she heard the noise, and for that she could only thank a moment of delightful inertia, of dreaming quiet—or her good luck. She had just finished two laps of the wurlie, one on the surface, one under the water, and she was catching her breath. She had retreated to a cool crevice beneath an overhang of the rock when the sound broke, either a human or animal sound. It must be an animal, for she had heard no human type of approach, no car, no cycle, anthing like that. Yet she had heard a noise, so how—what——

She peered out and almost laughed aloud. It was a horse. About to swim out and enjoy herself again, Georgina

51

stopped. The horse was not a wild one, no brumby, it was formally saddled, which meant ... *which meant* ...

It was then that she saw the foot.

It was a very large foot, undoubtedly belonging to a very large person. The foot was encased in a big, expensive-looking tan riding boot.

She could only see the foot, nothing else, and as this was the case she knew that the owner of the foot could not see her.

She shrank back beneath the overhang, thanking the northern latitudes for the water that was warm enough for her to remain there without bodily discomfort. She stayed quite still, for the slightest movement would have caused a ripple, and a ripple on this calm pool would have been an instant betrayal.

Keep quiet. Barely breathe. Don't move, she kept mentally briefing herself. Remember what you're wearing, and that's nothing at all.

The foot did not retreat. Was the fellow going to stand there for ever? Was he turned to stone? Thank goodness she had put the bike in a thicket, something she had always done as a matter of course, and thank goodness, too, her clothes were under a rock.

Still he stood. Then he must have picked up some pebbles, for he threw them into the water and the little waves came bounding at her, inundating her. Georgina, who out of caution had sunk even deeper with only her nose and eyes above the surface, could barely stop a splutter.

Go, go, go, she was willing the man, why don't you go?

Then the frog arrived. A big green frog. It came from somewhere under the rock and it landed on Georgina's nose, right on the tip of her nose. She looked at the frog and it looked back at her with unmoving black eyes. It probably thinks my nose is a leaf, or a lily pad, or something, Georgina realised, because I'm keeping so still. If I shudder it will leap and I shall scream, I couldn't help but scream. But then I mustn't shudder. I mustn't do anything.

Oh, please, up there, go.

At last the wearer of the boot did go.

Georgina saw the horse being deprived of its tasty cropping, saw the boot disappear as its owner evidently pulled himself into the saddle again. Then she heard the horse gallop off, the hooves soft on the new soft flood grass. No wonder she had not heard its approach, the animal would have trodden in silence on carpet-soft grass like this. But it didn't matter now, for she was free at last, free to dislodge the frog, free to get out.

Bare, shivering from her fright if not from the water, Georgina was out of the wurlie and into her clothes in record time. That she was still wet, dripping wet, did not occur to her. She simply pulled on shirt and pants.

She was racing back to the concealed cycle, kicking it to life again, then racing home to the hut as fast as she could.

Had she looked around her as she approached the chalet she would have seen a horse tethered behind the tank. But Georgina did not see; she only saw, when she entered the small brown room, a man waiting. He was sitting at the table and evidently watching her.

He wore large tan riding boots.

CHAPTER FIVE

'MR BROWN, I presume.' The big man sitting in front of her papers did not get up, and it took a few confused moments for Georgina to realise why, to remember she was a young man and not a young lady, and that older men do not rise for junior members of their own sex.

Not far from hysterical laughter, Georgina nearly retorted: 'No, I'm Dr Livingstone.'

She stopped it in time, though, and murmured: 'Yes, sir. Mr Roper, I presume.' She hoped she didn't sound facetious, and that he would not take it as effrontery.

He did not. He extended his large hand, so she extended hers, and the next moment she was biting back tears of pain. Quite unconscious of her torture of crushed bones—she was sure they were crushed—the big man waved magnanimously to the bed for Georgina to sit down, since there was only one chair in the hut, and he occupied it.

'How have you settled, Brown?' he asked.

His use of the surname irritated Georgina. It was not an Australianism; Australians were immediately on first name terms. An ordinary Australian would have called her George by this, asked her to call him Larry. Age made no difference, environment, status, still surnames were never used. Yet this extraordinary man chose to saw 'Brown', in a subtly condescending way. No wonder Craig had spoken of him as 'the mighty Roper'.

'I've settled well, sir,' she managed, 'I'm very comfortable.'

'And have been getting through some work, I see.' The man was turning over the pages that Georgina had stacked on the writing end of the table.

'Yes, sir.'

There was water trickling down her neck to her back from her wet hair; it was very uncomfortable.

The big man must have noticed it, for he said: 'You look hot and bothered. Feeling the weather up here?'

'It's hotter than Windmill Junction, sir.'

'I can see that by the state of your head. Your hair is drenched. See to it that you wear a hat, Brown.'

'Yes, sir. I had a helmet on just now. I was on the cycle.'

'Keep the helmet on while you're on wheels, of course, but carry a hat for when you're not. Obviously you're not used to the sun.'

'Oh, but I am, this dampness is because——' Georgina stopped herself sharply. 'I just hurried too much,' she excused instead.

'What was the rush?' he inquired.

'I—I'd thought of something I needed to jot down.'

'Then jot it down, man.' Roper tossed the notebook in front of him to Georgina, and followed it smartly with a pen. She was relieved that she caught both but not relieved to see that he was waiting for her to write. All her other notes were typed, intentionally typed so that her handwriting would not give her away. She scribbled something unintelligible, hoping to get out of it that way.

Now the water was running down her legs into her shoes, and Georgina knew that if she got up she would drip, and that if she bent she would squelch. She should have dried herself first with a handkerchief, or her neckerchief, or at least mopped up the surplus before she dressed. She gave a quick glance down to the floor; there was quite a pool there. So that he wouldn't see it she put her feet over it, then wondered if that was a good move, for her feet were small rather than large, and the sides of the lake on the floor still showed.

Fortunately he was not looking. He was turning over her stepfather's manuscript, or rather her manuscript on her stepfather's notes. 'An interesting thesis,' he nodded. 'May I ask the source?'

'Of the author of the subject?' she hedged.

'Yes.'

'His name was Iain Sutherland. He—he has passed on now.'

'Odd, I've never heard of him,' he said thoughtfully.

'You wouldn't unless you were a student.'

'Of geology?'

'Yes,' she nodded.

'Would a graduate do?' he drawled idly.

Georgina was startled. 'Are you, sir?'

'Naturally.'

'I'm sorry, I just thought with all your cattle that this'— she glanced at the reports she had made for him—'might be a sideline, a hobby.'

'The cattle is my sideline. I inherited it and I intend to preserve it, but geology is my interest. No, I don't know your man. I'll say this, though, you're certainly presenting a very interesting angle of him. Why, even the layman would want to read this.' He flicked the pages.

'Thank you.' Georgina hastened to correct herself. 'Thanks, I mean, to Iain Sutherland's inspiration. I think I'm the first one to choose him as a subject.' She did not think, she knew. Stepfather had been so long away from university walls that no one would have remembered him.

'Yet praise to you, too, in your interpretation of him,' Roper awarded. 'Do you know, Brown, your writing would even attract a woman, and women notoriously shy away from things like that. Yes, you have a definite understanding of females.'

'Yes, sir,' Georgina said. She was only half-listening because she had just heard a drip. It came from her crossed knees where the soaked denim formed droplets that plinked when they fell. She uncrossed her knees.

'Met the men yet?' Larry Roper asked next.

'We've yarned over the sliprail,' she said.

'That won't do, you'll have to go over for a beer. You'll have to have a poker game with the boys.'

'Well, I don't know whether I could, sir. I mean, I'm kept busy. I want to go out after more evidence for you, and then my thesis is due.' She eyed him nervously.

'Very admirable, I'm sure, but all work and no play makes—George'—a short laugh—'a dull boy. We don't want you dull, do we, George Brown?'

'No, sir.'

'Then think about it. A healthy mind in a healthy body, and all that.' Larry Roper's voice stopped short, and wretchedly Georgina looked up, imagining all kinds of things, to become more wretched still. She should never have done it, but it was too late now; she had, and it was done. She had gathered a handful of Salvation Jane and put the handful into an empty jam-jar. Shrinkingly she turned her eyes from the unbelievable blue of the desert flowers to look at him. His eyes were the same blue, she saw. But not just that, they were at this moment sympathetic. The mighty Roper sympathetic? Sympathetic, anyway, when it came to flowers!

'Keen on botany, too, Brown?' he asked.

'Well——'

'Nothing to be ashamed of, it's a poor man who can't find time in his life for a flower. You'll see a lot more tomorrow. I'm taking you out to the Lucy to show you some indications I found that seem quite promising. That's where you'll really find the floral wonderland.'

'Is the Lucy far, sir? I've been looking for it.' Thankfully Georgina left the subject of flowers.

'Then you've been looking in the wrong direction, for it's only an hour's run. At the height of the Wet it even lapped that outcrop out here.' He pointed. 'Probably you were looking the other way, it's very easy to do that out here. Now, how about letting the homestead get to know you better over dinner tonight?'

'I already know Mrs Willmott,' she hedged.

'I'll be there as well this time,' he pointed out.

'If you don't mind, sir, I have a few things to do.'

'I do mind,' Roper said it sharply.

'But it wasn't required, was it?' said Georgina equally sharply, before she could remember where she was and what—most importantly—what she was supposed to be. 'It wasn't down among the requirements to be social,' she said more mildly.

'No, but then lots of details aren't included in a list of requirements—just as lots of things that the applicant has to offer are left out.' His voice was unemotional. 'However, please yourself.'

'Thank you, sir.'

Georgina followed Larry Roper to the door. Curiosity made her say: 'I didn't hear you land, sir.'

'Land?'

'Mrs Willmott said you would fly up,' she explained.

'I landed at the Brydens', due north of here, and wangled transport down, four-legged variety.' He nodded to the horse.

'Brydens'——?'

'They've leased the place from Everson, otherwise I wouldn't have put down there, at least not if he was around, even though our own fields are all in use until the road train arrives to transport the beasts south.'

So, thought Georgina, Craig has left. If I want to see him, if I need to, it will have to be on his next run, though he has told me that if the worst comes to the worst I can stay at his old home.

'See you, Brown.' The big man crossed to the horse, pulled himself on and was lost at once in the cloud of dust which covered the track that led up to the house.

Georgina went back into the hut and wasted no time in changing. It was only as she was drying her hair that she remembered Roper's conversation ... at least part of his conversation. That 'lots of things that the applicant has to offer are left out'. Could that mean ... could he suspect ...

58

No, she decided, he had no inkling at all.

She sat down at the table where he had sat, read what he had read. 'You have a definite understanding of females.' She heard it again. But he had offered it in praise, she was sure of that.

It was unfortunate that he had arrived so soon, but she decided now she could do nothing about it. She had meant to slip quietly out the day before he came back, but to slip quietly out the day after would present some difficulties. For instance, between here and the road there was the big house to pass, and where before there only had been Mrs Willmott to show a cup of tea, now there was the mighty Roper. Showing authority.

Anyway, she wasn't finished here yet. She did not wish to leave. Until she did, why not ... yes, *why not* stay on? In spite of that 'lots of things are left out' of Larry Roper's, Georgina felt sure he hadn't suspected, had not the smallest suspicion. He was a very self-absorbed man. What notice, what possible notice would he take of an insignificant underling like her?

Yes, I will stay, she resolved. I will stay at least until my first pay, which I will send down to Joanne as an instalment. She looked at the typewriter, looked at her typed findings, her typed manuscript. At least, she thought, he will never know about me through that. He has heard my voice, and not known, he has discussed things with me and not suspected. With ordinary luck I can keep it like that, and anyhow I'm going to have a jolly good try.

On which note Georgina opened the sherry again, and smiled as she made a toast.

'To mighty Roper—the bigger they are the harder they fall!' If only, she giggled, the mighty Roper had known how nearly she had fallen as she stared back one bare inch into the eye of a frog!

When Larry Roper came down the next morning in a jeep, Georgina was ready in her jeans, loose shirt and crash helmet.

'You won't need that,' Roper indicated the helmet, 'you're travelling with me in the wagon. But bring a hat.'

'I won't need that either, I'm used to the sun.'

'So it appeared by your sweat yesterday. Hat, Brown.' His voice was stern.

Georgina said wisely: 'Very well, sir.'

She also brought her tools, including the magnet all geologists carried, some coloured ribbons for marking, and a notebook and pencil.

'Best throw in a towel,' advised Roper lazily, 'you might like to dip in the Lucy.'

'In that case I'll——' But Georgina remembered in time that she could *not* include a bikini, so said instead: 'No, I don't think I will.' She added lamely: 'I have a cold.'

'I thought you were sweating too much yesterday. I'll take you up to the house when we come back and give you a double rum. You seem to be better now, though,' he was estimating her, 'your hair's dried off. It was soaked when you came in. Do you always wear it so short? Rather a change from the fellows these days.'

She swallowed. 'I . . . yes, I do.'

'I'm not complaining,' he said. 'Hop in.'

They struck out into the desert, and if there was a track, Georgina could not see it.

'What was Windmill Junction like?' he asked idly as they bumped along.

'One windmill and no junction,' she responded, 'I thought it was frontier country until I saw this.'

'Go north-west again and you'll call this Piccadilly,' he grinned. He steered the jeep through a thicket of bush comprising ironwood, gidgee, some tamarisks and actually a few tropical palms. Georgina called out in surprised delight at the palms, for she had not expected them, but when they emerged to the desert again she was silent with disbelief, for the palmy retreat, welcome as it had been, was nothing to the sudden flood of blossom that awaited them, sand gorse in shining gold, Indian daisies in purest white, and, of course, the ever-present Salvation Jane. That bluest of all blues, the Jane.

'A garden, isn't it?' said Roper. He pointed to a small lagoon on their right, its stretch of sparkling water busy with insects weaving gauzy patterns above it. There was a river smell, somehow, making Georgina feel that the Lucy could not be far away.

She asked Roper, and he nodded. 'But only an anabranch,' he said.

'What's that?'

'An anabranch is a stream that leaves the river and later re-enters it. I'm afraid that's all the Lucy you'll see this time, Brown, unless you travel many more kilometres, which I don't propose to do. During the Wet this anabranch is part of the Lucy's inland ocean, for it is almost that, with waves four feet deep.'

But the water when they reached it was waveless, very still, very limpid and very inviting.

'Going to sample it?' the man called.

'No, I've got a cold. I told you so.'

'I never knew a cold yet that didn't benefit from water. Well, I'm going in.' Stepping out of the jeep, Roper began pulling off his shirt.

Georgina was out of the wagon in a flash, but even then he was up to the stage of unbuckling his belt.

'A blackbutt,' she called desperately and deceitfully, for there was not a blackbutt in sight, 'now that could be a sign of nickel.' Before he could comment she was hurrying into the scrub.

She heard the water splash as he dived in, and pretended deep intrigue in something in the ground.

'It's fine,' he called out. 'Change your mind, Brown.'

'Next time,' she answered, finding a necessity to peer further and closer to the ground. She wondered how long he would swim.

She stayed there until she felt that to stay there any longer would invite a comment. She straightened slowly

61

and turned round.

He was out and dressed up to his waist. He had very big, very brown shoulders, she saw. He had draped his towel over the jeep bonnet to dry, and now he strolled across to her.

'What school did you go to, Brown?' he asked.

For an hysterical moment Georgina wondered what would happen if she answered: 'St Hilda's.'

'I ... well, mostly I had correspondence lessons,' she evaded.

'I gathered so.' His tone was dry. 'Like the nickel you were pretending to look for, there are signs.'

'Signs of what, sir?'

'Forget it,' he said brusquely. 'I mean forget it now. But later on I think we'll have to do something about you, Brown.'

'Something, sir?' Uneasiness gripped her.

'Did you bring your magnet with you?' He ignored her question. 'Then look for some outcrops and see if you can feel a pull. Watch for the light brown silica, it's a possible trap.'

'I know all that.' Georgina said it indignantly.

'Well, the way you were behaving while I took my swim would have fooled me,' he said acidly, 'you had the magnet the wrong way round. Anyway, we'll forget it all now and eat instead—that dip made me hungry. Get a fire going.'

'Yes, sir.' This at least was something she could do, and after she had gathered tinder and lit it, added some telling chunks of wood and had the satisfaction of seeing a good fire catch on, she said happily, happy that she had succeeded at least with this: 'I should have thought you would have been a flask man, Mr Roper, I shouldn't have thought you would waste your time on a fire.'

'Wasted?' he said, and he inhaled a deep breath. Georgina did, too, and took in that unforgettable tang of smouldering bark, redolent wood and herby twigs.

He tossed her a bag of flour. 'Can you make a damper?'

'Of course.'

He watched her do it. 'Actually,' he told her, 'you should use ash for rising, but you seem to know what you're about. In fact, Brown, you have quite the light touch, the kind of touch you mostly see in female cooks.' He grinned, and Georgina supposed she had better grin back. She hoped the grin did not look as sickly as she felt, but the damper was a success.

They separated after lunch, both with their magnets and their markers.

Georgina found an intrusive and was examining it with absorption when she heard him shout.

'Over here, Brown, I have a little job for you.'

'Yes, sir.'

It was some time before Georgina met Roper. In the emptiness of the desert the voice seemed to lose direction, and he had to call twice. She wondered what he wanted; he had not sounded excited, as a find would make you excited.

She reached him at last. Perhaps he had noticed some semi-precious stuff like topaz or jasper, of no great value but of interest, and he wanted to show her.

But the mighty Roper did not want to show anything like that.

'Look,' he said, and Georgina looked. Her stomach heaved.

There was a waterhole with a carcase half in it, half out. 'The poor beast,' said Roper, 'must have got bogged there in the mud following the Wet.'

'Y-yes,' gulped Georgina.

'It's a hazard,' Roper said. 'What water will still remain in the hole when the Dry finally comes will be badly polluted. A human life could be lost.'

Something more was coming; Georgina sensed it, and did not like what she sensed.

'But no one,' she said faintly, 'would drink such water.'

'Ah,' he came back, and with it he shot out an accusing finger, 'I expected that. But we don't do things that way,

Brown, not at Roper's. You may have at Windmill Junction, I don't know.'

'At Windmill there were no beasts—I mean no bogged beasts,' she defended.

'Then good for you, for as you see there are here.'

'No one would drink from it,' Georgina insisted.

'If they were parched?' His voice probed.

'These days everyone knows the law of survival.' Georgina knew she was babbling but she knew, too, that she had to. She had to stop—or at least defer—something that seemed very likely to happen, and happen to her.

'You always carry a sheet of plastic,' she cried, and it was very like a cry for help.

'Go on,' he advised.

'You dig in the soil, and you . . . Oh, everyone knows.'

'Yes,' he nodded, 'even you. But I still think a pure pool of water would be more satisfactory.'

'Of course it would be if you needed it, but you wouldn't need it here. You could go to the anabranch of the river.'

'In a fever for water you could miss the river. Indeed, it has been done. Anyway in the Dry the anabranch could be reduced to a few feet, or it might not even be there at all. Only a pool of water could stand between you and death, only it still would be death, a worse death if it's left like this. So, Brown, we do what human decency demands. We remove the danger. Attend to this carcase at once.' His face was grim.

'Me?' she asked faintly.

'I'm not looking at anyone else.'

'W-what do you want done with it?'

'Well, I can tell you I don't want it stuffed for dinner.'

Again Georgina's stomach heaved.

'No, I want it removed and buried.'

'I have no spade,' she pointed out.

'You can bury it in a cleft and place some shrubs and roots on top. Now get to it, man.'

64

'It's very large,' Georgina said faintly.

'But not much weight any more,' Roper replied cheerfully.

Georgina swallowed. 'Can I come back later? With precision work like mine I have to preserve my hands. I'd need to wear gloves.'

'I have gloves,' he offered.

'They'd be too large.'

'You can tie them on with some of the marker ribbons if you like, but what *I* would like is some action, Brown. While you're considering it you could have got it done. Now, get to it.'

'Yes,' Georgina said.

She took a step forward. If only, she thought miserably, the poor beast had bogged himself some months before he had. It wouldn't have been so bad just handling bones; bad enough, but—but this!

Another step. Another revulsion.

Another step ... then a heave she simply could not stop. She ran into the bush, and there she stood until the attack was over. She would try again, she told herself. There simply couldn't be anything left inside her.

She went wretchedly back until she reached the waterhole, then she stopped. It was empty.

'Yes, I've done it.' Roper came and stood beside her. 'If anyone poisons himself where I've put it, then he deserves his bad luck.'

'Thank you, sir.'

'It wasn't a pleasant job, and I don't blame you for throwing up, but good lord, boy, you have to think of others. Keep that in mind next time.'

Next time! Georgina vowed she would be away from this place by then.

'We'll get back now. I could do with a hot scour after that and then a long, strong tot of rum. How about you?'

'I think I'll stay at home, sir.'

'I rather think so, too. You haven't done so well today,

have you, so why should I waste a rum on you or your cold? Or is it nausea now? Are you prone to illness?' He looked hard at her. 'Even if you are, you can still drive back, Brown. I'll sit behind, I don't want to start you heaving again with any odour I have accumulated.'

'No, sir,' she said tonelessly.

They did not speak on the return journey. Several times Roper indicated the direction, but that was all.

When they got to the hut and Georgina climbed out of the jeep and Roper took her place, Roper asked: 'Brown, just why did you come out here?'

'To—to Roper's?' she asked.

'Yes, Brown.'

'I answered your advertisement.'

'Yes, but why?' he insisted.

'I knew I'd like it—I liked where I was, so I knew I would like this place more.'

'And now?' Roper asked.

'Now I still do, sir. I mean—Well, we can't all be the same, sir.'

'I agree. But you know, Brown, I have a feeling that you're a great deal different from me.'

'You mean because I get nauseated?'

'That—among other things,' he said enigmatically.

'I'm sorry, sir.'

'Well, we'll see about it later, I think.' Roper was at the controls now and he drove off so quickly that Georgina was left standing there.

But not for long. Going into the hut, she shut and then locked it, then she draped the windows with anything she could find, and filled the bath dish to the brim. She, too, intended to wash off the smell of the poor bogged beast. She emerged at last, well soaped, well scrubbed but still greenish, yet with her mind made up.

I can't go through with it, she thought. I'll leave tonight.

CHAPTER SIX

GEORGINA packed the few things she would need at the Brydens' until Craig could pick her up and take her south with him, then the rest she bundled neatly and placed behind the door to be called for later. She would have to travel to Craig's old home by cycle, and it could be up to a hundred kilometres away, perhaps more, so there was no question of any large luggage; there must be strictly only essentials, and they would have to fit on the back of the bike.

After packing and unpacking several exasperating times she made the bundle small enough to stow into a haversack to be shoved behind the seat, but even then it looked conspicuous, and all she could hope was that she met no one, or if she did, that in the dark—it must get dark sometime—they would not notice her.

Whom she meant by 'they', Georgina shrank from analysing.

Good manners obliged her to leave a note. Since there was no need to try to live a lie now, she simply penned, not typed it.

'Dear Mr Roper, I am sorry if I have inconvenienced you, but I feel I cannot stay here any longer. If the things I have left behind are a hindrance, or if you need the hut, please put them outside. I will remove them at my first opportunity. Regarding the cycle, it will be returned in good order and refuelled. Thank you. G. Brown.'

She decided not to elaborate on that 'G'. He could come to any conclusion he liked.

Everything was done at last, and she went and sat at the

door. She wished the sun would stop balancing on the horizon. She always loved this poised moment before curtains, as it were, the rising climax to night, but this evening she could have pushed the sun over the edge in her impatience to be gone.

At last, in its usual over-abundance of colour it sank, and at once the blue of evening came in. She would allow a few minutes more to let the blue deepen, then she would push off.

She looked around her at the hut she had occupied so briefly. It was absurd, but already it had come to mean something to her. Her tenseness after her stepfather's death had left her here, and she had begun to come to terms with herself. Until he, Roper, had come she had known a relaxation she had not known for weeks. Yes, she had been well on the way to loving this little brown strictly masculine room. She saw that she had left the jam jar of Salvation Jane still there, so she emptied it and put the jar away.

It was getting darker now. Ordinarily she would have lit the lamp by this and soaked up the corner shadows, but as she would be leaving quite soon it wasn't worth while.

Yes—looking around again—she'd been happy here, that is until the arrival of the mighty Roper. It was his right to come, for after all he owned it, but just as he had spoiled Craig's life and Elva's life, he had spoiled this period of her life. Some people were like that, they spoiled things. Mighty Roper, the spoiler! she said to the quickening dusk, and, deciding it was time now, she got up and went out, shut the door behind her on her stacked belongings, then crossed to where she always propped the cycle against the tank stand. She mounted and kicked off, but once the engine sparked she accelerated very cautiously. She only intended to ride until she saw the lights of the homestead, then she would push quietly past the property until she had left Roper's safely behind, and could afford to mount again, make more noise and speed away.

When the glow of the colonial house greeted her, and she

stopped the engine, got off and began to push, she found the going dismayingly hard. The ground was not suitable for the manual manipulation of a bike; the motorcycle proved far heavier than she had thought. Riding the thing had been uncomfortable, but pushing, she found, was torture. She could feel beads of sweat on her brow, and knew that if *he* were here he would suggest a rum, since it appeared after all that she did have that cold.

But for all the backbreaking work that the shoving entailed, Georgina pushed on, silently she trusted, peering blindly into the darkness ahead of her and yearning for the moment she could leap on the bike again and open up.

But the time did not come, for instead a man came—or at least a male figure rose up before her, just as she was parallel to the house.

'Our young Mr Brown, no less,' called Larry Roper. 'Now this is an unexpected pleasure. Mrs Willmott was very disappointed when I told her you'd declined the dinner invitation. "That boy needs feeding up," she said, "I don't think he bothers about himself." I came outside just now, toying with the idea of going down and trying to persuade you to change your mind, and here you are of your own accord, and visiting us just as we asked.' He smiled at Georgina.

'Yes, sir,' Georgina said. What else could she say? 'I rode up in case——' She stopped. She had been about to say: 'I rode up in case you felt obliged to escort me back afterwards and I didn't want you to have that trouble.' But she remembered in time that she was George, and the Georges don't get escorted home, only Georginas.

'In case the walk there and back knocked you out?' he nodded feelingly. 'It's a fair step, and I can see now that you do have a chill; why, you're all wet again, Brown. Yes, a double rum tonight for you.'

'I wouldn't be able to ride after that!' Georgina tried to protest friskily, or however men sounded when they protested something they did not mean.

'Well, we'll put a toddy in a flask for you and give it to

you to take back. We'll have to beat that cold. Come on in, son.' Roper led the way into the house.

They sat in the front room and Larry Roper poured two whiskies as Mrs Willmott, delighted to see George, fussed with the dinner. The room was just as Georgina had heard north-west lounges, or sitting rooms, were; it was large, airy, and had polished green cement slabs for coolness underfoot, and mostly bamboo furnishings.

'Too strong?' asked Roper of Georgina's Scotch.

'Oh, no, sir,' Georgina assured him hurriedly. If she had told the truth she would have said that it was too everything. She hated whisky, and she was acutely aware that she had to keep a cool head and weigh every word before it was spoken, and spirits weren't exactly conducive to that.

'I'm very pleased to have you here, Brown,' Larry Roper began genially. 'I've always had jackeroos—there've been a few in your hut before you—but this is the first time I've had a geologist. I told you before that my real interest is the earth itself and what's in it, not what's on it, like crops or stock. But I have to keep faith with my forefathers, I wouldn't be deserving of Roper's if I didn't. Anyway, I have no real dislike of the pastoralist's life, indeed, I have a mild love for it. But the possibility of the other is my dream. I look out and try to think of it all in ten years' time when the drillers and what-have-yous have taken over the place, when the technocrats come in with their delicate instruments, when the first percussion points reach the core.'

'It won't be so—pleasant.' Georgina had started to say 'beautiful', but changed it to pleasant as somehow more masculine.

'It depends on how you see it,' Roper shrugged. 'Some might see gargantuan monsters in wires and cranes and derricks, but I see a kind of romance.'

He looked at her keenly. 'But don't think if it all comes off that it means an end to what I inherited. Oh, no, young Brown, the pastoral side only makes my success in what's under the earth a bigger challenge. I'm going to prove that

70

the two extremes, the mining man and the pastoralist—in other words the downstairs and the upstairs man—can live together. There's always been friction between them, you know. Holes left in the ground by the geos to break a beast's leg are a basis for complaint on the pastoral side, endless adverse reports from the farmer concerning the geo and his work which he feels he doesn't deserve. Well, I aim to stop all that. Drink up, Brown.' He himself drank, then crossed to the bar to refill his glass. Georgina, looking around for a flowerpot, that oldest escape of all, found none, so crossed to the window ostensibly to observe the night. While she was there she hurriedly emptied her glass.

'Not a bad drop, is it?' Roper was standing beside her already. 'Best imported Hieland dew. Lucky to get it.' Was it Georgina's imagination, or was he looking fixedly through the darkness at a damp patch that he couldn't possibly see?

'It's a lovely night,' Georgina diverted him hurriedly. 'You have a good view here.'

'Of darkness,' he agreed, 'the same as you.' He still seemed to be looking at something.

'Dinner!' It was Mrs Willmott, and Georgina could have kissed her.

They went into a big raftered dining room.

'One night you'll have to eat with the boys,' Larry Roper said. 'I do it quite often myself. There are none of the fancy candles that Willy here loves to bring out but they do have a good cook. They play snooker or poker afterwards, or, if you prefer, a yarn.' He studied her for a moment.

'Anyway,' Roper resumed, 'although you're here as a geo, I'd like you to see the cattle side of the story, and hear what the men have to say. I don't want you to be narrow-minded, Brown.'

'No, sir.'

Mrs Willmott was watching Georgina's plate keenly. At any minute, Georgina thought, she would remark: 'You have the appetite of a girl.'

Georgina began shovelling the food into her, until,

glancing up suddenly, she found Roper looking at her.

'Tuck in, son,' he said, and he smiled paternally on Georgina—but there was something malicious as well as paternal there. Something Georgina could not put a finger on.

After two helpings of pudding, Georgina felt she could have lain down and slept. However, Mrs Willmott was well pleased, and when Roper went out, saying he would be back soon, the housekeeper became very expansive.

She told Georgina she had been with Mr Larry for years. A wonderful man. Look how he had gone out just now— he saw each of his men every night. She had no doubt he would do the same with George.

Georgina flinched.

Her glance fell on the large sideboard and on three photos of three different girls. Mrs Willmott followed her gaze.

'No wonder,' she said acidly, 'he turned out as antagonistic to women as he did.'

'But three of them!' Georgina exclaimed involuntarily.

'Four, actually, but *she* isn't displayed—oh, no. Now I'll see to the dishes, George.'

'Can I help you?'

'Help me?' Mrs Willmott looked shocked.

'Men do,' defended Georgina.

'Not here. You just sit down and rest.'

Resting was the last thing Georgina wanted to do; she wanted to walk a mile after that meal. Instead she crossed to the sideboard and looked again at the photos.

'It must seem like a harem to you.' Larry Roper had come back to the room again and crossed to stand beside her. 'Gina, Libby, Melinda.' He introduced them in turn. 'May they never darken my door again!'

'You sound serious,' she said.

'I've never been more serious in my life.'

'Are they the reason that you hate women?' Georgina said spontaneously.

'Who said I hate women?' he demanded.

'Your telegram to me.' Georgina nearly said: 'Also you let it be known across the telephone in no uncertain words.'

'If I recall,' he came in, 'all I wrote in that wire was "No women here".'

'You said definitely none,' Georgina corrected. She would have liked to add: 'And you said over the phone "A what?" when Bill said I was what I was.' 'Which one,' she asked instead, 'was the last straw?'

He shrugged at that. 'They all were, but the real culmination isn't there. Unfortunately I'm obliged to have the others.'

Obliged? Curiouser and curiouser, thought Georgina, feeling as puzzled as Alice in Wonderland.

'You're an inquisitive boy, Brown.' Roper was regarding Georgina narrowly now.

Something took hold of her. 'Because I ask you about three pretty girls? Why can't I admire them?' She knew she was speaking incautiously, but somehow she couldn't help herself. 'After all, Mr Roper, I'm not so old myself.'

It was a stupid remark, a remark that opened up something, and she regretted it instantly. Larry Roper drawled at once: 'I can see we must have some parties and find you some nice company, George. As you point out, why not? Yes, I'll get on to that.'

Now Georgina did not answer.

Mrs Willmott took coffee into the lounge and Roper and Georgina followed. Talk was general for a while, with Georgina watching herself closely and going very carefully with the brandy that was served with the coffee. It would be fatal to answer Mrs Willmott or Mr Roper in her own language and not the language of men. Then Mrs Willmott excused herself, and the real talk of the evening began, talk that Georgina had dreaded but soon enjoyed, just as she had enjoyed it in Windmill Junction. Yet Windmill had only been elementary compared to what Roper talked about now.

He told her of his mining beginnings, of the rocks that

73

used to be thrown contemptuously away as rubbish when he was a boy, and the significant metals they had changed to today.

He talked graphically, and took Georgina with him every stony inch of the way. No longer was she a man, nor was she for that matter a woman, she was instead a child, wide-eyed, enthralled; she was a student sitting enchanted at his feet.

'You're a good audience, Brown,' he said once. 'Heaven knows I've wanted to talk like this. I needed it. I like my men, but I wanted someone who speaks my own language, shares my love.

'My father,' he went on, 'was tolerant of my enthusiasm for minerals but not enthusiastic. Cattle were in his blood. He never stopped me in my ambitions, but he let me know that I was on my own in this and that he wouldn't join me—financially was what he really meant. I studied till my eyes couldn't follow another line, and I worked like a dog. Then I snared a job with a big company with wealthy equipment, top men with know-how, and I don't mind telling you I picked their brains.' He grinned at Georgina. 'I breathed maps, lived charts and saved for every three hundred dollars it takes to peg a claim and for every seven dollars a foot it takes to drill it. It had to be my own money, my father had said that.'

'And now you have it all wrapped up as near as your own front door,' Georgina came in, and he nodded.

'I believe so. I've always believed so, but first I had to be sure. I was broke by the time my father died and I duly inherited Roper's ... broke in cash but not in know-how. Now'—he turned fully and smiled at her—'it's all waiting for the picking, I believe, and I thank you, Brown, believe that with me.'

'Yes,' Georgina said.

'That dustbowl outside—not dust now but it will be again—is waiting for the big squeeze, the squeeze that will bring out what I know it's concealing. Then it will all start,

Brown. You'll be mapping, structure interpreting, pit sampling. I'll be bringing up diggers from the city, or buying them from other projects, and forming the gangs. We'll be drilling.' His blue eyes were shining, and Georgina thought with surprise:

'Why, he's young!'

'But in all that time,' he continued steadily, 'the station has to go on. The men, my dad's men, a few of the old-timers who were here even when my grandfather was boss, have to be allowed their side. Tomorrow, Brown, you'll see that side. Do you ride?'

'Yes, sir, but——' She broke off as he smiled.

'But not so well? Not to worry about that. It wasn't one of my stipulations. I'll see you get a reasonable mount.'

'Thank you, sir,' she said gratefully.

'And now I'll drive you back to the hut. It's late enough if we're to do what I plan for tomorrow.' He rose.

'Oh, no,' protested Georgina, 'I have the bike here.'

'I'm aware of that, but I'm aware, too, of how hazardous it is to ride down that track at night with only two wheels. Actually I don't know how you got up here without a fall.'

Georgina could have told him that she had pushed the bike, but of course she didn't.

She said: 'I was all right before, I'll be all right now.'

'In the car you will,' he said tersely. 'You can collect the bike tomorrow.'

Yes, with a large haversack strapped on to it, a conspicuous and significant haversack, Georgina thought. That meant that she would have to get up very early in the morning and remove the bike before he saw.

She went out and thanked Mrs Willmott, then came back to where Roper waited in the hall.

'You're quite a nice-mannered boy, Brown,' he commented. 'Willy will appreciate that, she'll want you back next week.'

Heaven forbid, prayed Georgina.

'It all rather surprises me,' Roper went on as they went

out. 'Kids who are home-educated generally turn out spoiled and lacking in social graces. Boarding school licks one into shape, even though the licking often dries very quickly afterwards. You did say you were taught at home?'

'Well, I didn't go to any boys' school,' Georgina said truthfully.

'And I hardly think you went to a girls',' he laughed. Was it her imagination, Georgina wondered, or was it a laugh with another side to it? But she must have been edgy, for he led the way out, talking casually again. She got into the car beside him and he drove down to the hut. Thank heaven, Georgina sighed, that this nightmare was nearly over.

But it was not to be over yet.

Roper got out of the car when Georgina did instead of driving straight off. *Why* was he getting out of the car? Georgina panicked.

He even went as far as the hut with her. 'Did you bring a torch?' he asked. 'You always want to bring a flash. Try to remember there are no mod cons down here, like being able to switch on a light. Why, you could even have a snake coiled on the floor. And what in tarnation is wrong with the door? It seems to be jammed. No, there's something against it.'

She took a deep breath. 'I was cleaning up and I put my things at one end ... that end. Then—then I decided I didn't feel like cleaning, so I took you up on that invitation instead.'

'And I'm pleased you did, Brown—you were welcome. I'll see you tomorrow then, and I'll show you how the other side ticks. Sleep tight.'

'Yes, Mr Roper. Goodnight.' Georgina stood at the door until he left.

Sleep tight? she said incredulously to herself, sleep tight with the knowledge that she had to be up at the homestead to collect the bike before cockcrow, or whatever it was that woke people up out here?

76

Not bothering to light the lamp and soak up any shadows, for no lamp could have soaked up her shadows just now, Georgina undressed quickly and jumped into bed.

Anxiety not to sleep too far into the next day resulted in her not sleeping at all. She was hollow-eyed as she pulled on her jeans and loose shirt, then began the trek to the homestead. She watched the house for some time, but when no sign of life showed, and when piccaninny daylight showed dangerous signs of fading even further, she moved forward.

Everything went well. She was able to move the bike—haversack still intact—away from where she had propped it last night and take it back to the hut again.

She was exhausted when she got there, and a quick glance in the speckled mirror showed a pale, shadowy-eyed boy. She shuddered to think what kind of show she would make on horseback today. But perhaps with an hour's sleep ...

But even that was denied her at first. Behind her in the mirror she saw the bags and parcels she had placed in readiness to be picked up after she had left here. About to put them all back again, she saw that something was missing. It was that note she had written and left on top, that: 'Dear Mr Roper, I'm sorry ...' She was sure she had placed it on the bags.

Piece by piece she re-stacked the luggage and made the hut look as it had looked prior to her decision to leave. When he came down later with her mount for today he might wonder if the bags were still there, might even look closer.

But still she found no note. Perhaps it had blown away; perhaps it had blown under the table, blown beneath the bed——

The bed. Suddenly so weary she could not think of anything else any longer, Georgina tottered across to the bed and flopped down.

The next thing she knew was a knock on the door and a

sound that could only be a horse's hoof.

'Rise and shine!' Roper called out. 'I'm waiting, young Brown.'

Georgina dragged herself up, pulled a comb through her hair and called: 'Coming, sir!'

CHAPTER SEVEN

THE horse was a reasonable size and did not look too forbidding. If she had had a fair night's sleep she would have looked forward to climbing up and cantering into the herby scrub beside the mighty Roper, Georgina thought, but drained as she was——

But once beside her mount she put every bit of effort into her haul up and actually made it to her satisfaction. She trusted it was to Roper's satisfaction, too, but she did not look across at him to find out.

'His name is Ribbons,' Roper was advising her, 'probably because they knew he'd never get any. But he's a tolerant chap and shouldn't take off.'

'Take off?' she asked numbly.

'Into the bush if something upsets him. There's a lot to upset a mount out here. That, for instance.' Larry Roper pointed. 'That' was a gecko lizard, keeping absolutely quiet, pretending he wasn't there, something that lizards did very well. 'If the gecko was on the track and decided to move just as Ribbons put his foot down, it could be a different story,' he went on. 'I'm just telling you, Brown, so you won't let Ribbons' easy gait send you off into a doze, which you look as if you might do at any minute. What's wrong? Didn't you sleep last night?'

'Yes,' lied Georgina, 'but I guess I just need more sleep out here. I think' ... inspired ... 'I'll deprive myself of social evenings in the future and go to bed instead.'

'You'll get over that,' he dismissed. 'It's just the change of air.'

They rode indian-file through the thicker scrub then side

by side over a patch of gibber. When they came to some coarse grass, Roper let his own mount, Gibraltar, have his head, so Georgina supposed she had better do the same with Ribbons.

They rode on like that for perhaps an hour, then Roper drew Georgina's attention to a blur in the distance. He said it would be the mob.

They took another thirty minutes reaching it, this time over dry-as-old-hay terrain, despite the recent big Wet. Some terrain, Roper related, was like that, it never got enough rain. The two horses, whose enthusiasm had diminished somewhat at having sandy waste instead of grass under their hooves, had slackened pace, and now had to be scolded on.

They paused for a drink for the horses, a small wurlie this time, set in bluebush.

'I suppose you know all the drinking holes,' Georgina said with careful offhandedness, and he nodded.

'Every one. It's essential. I could tell if even one ripple had been unrippled.'

Or a frog dislodged? But Georgina did not say it. She moistened her hot face with her handkerchief dipped in the wurlie and wrung out, then mounted Ribbons once more.

They rode off again to the distant blur that was now taking the shape of a dust cloud which was formed, Roper said, by a thousand hooves.

'Is there no grass there?' she inquired.

'You put that many feet on grass and see what you finish up with,' he shrugged.

The cattlemen waved to them as they came up, but they also waved them away from the herd. The beasts were touchy this morning, they explained. There had been some brumby camels around, and sometimes that was all that was needed with these prima donnas. The stockmen suggested that they all ate further away on the hill.

The 'hill', like the 'valley' where her hut was, proved

equally level to Georgina, but the meal the men put on proved a great success. That the tea was brewed from the same water which boiled the scrubbed jacket potatoes didn't lessen its aroma, and the great slabs of brisket on Mrs Willmott's home-made bread was wonderful.

'What's wrong with the beasts?' Roper was stirring his tea with a twig.

'Just touchy. You know how they are, boss, sometimes you could drive a fire engine through them and they wouldn't stir, but today they're on edge.'

'There must be a reason, I mean apart from the camels. They generally take the camels fairly well—— Ah, I think that could be the reason now.' Roper pointed to the distance and there in the sky Georgina could see the silhouette of a small plane.

'Overhead noise is something they don't like,' Roper told Georgina. 'Camels I have no doubt they can explain to themselves in a kind of animal way, also harriers and hawks, but never monstrous birds like that. So long as the wretch doesn't come any closer.'

'I shouldn't think he would, boss,' one of the drovers advised, 'that sort isn't interested in beef on the hoof, only in what lies in the ground under the hoof.'

'Yes,' Roper agreed drily. He looked at Georgina. 'A spy plane,' he explained.

'I thought so,' she nodded.

Stomachs well filled, the cattlemen spread themselves out, leaving two on watch to guard the mob, and slept. Larry Roper did the same as a matter of course, and feeling she would be conspicuous by not following suit, Georgina stretched out, too.

She would have dearly have loved to have let herself sleep, or just drift off, but that was a luxury she must wait for until she reached the hut again and closed the door behind her.

It was difficult to stay awake, though; the sun was pouring down on them. No wonder, Georgina thought drowsily, that lizards fall asleep on sunbaked rocks. Also the herby smell of the desert was almost soporific, the occasional ring of a hoof and the occasional cry of a harrier almost mesmeric. But no, she must not sleep. Sleep out here would be dangerous. She could say something, and it could be a wrong thing . . . for a George.

She opened her eyes and flicked her glance round. Everyone else slept soundly. If she got up it might break this longing for sleep; she could move around, walk somewhere. If Roper saw her she could always say she was looking for signs.

But it was too risky to get up here, the men were too close to her. *He* was too close. She looked at him covertly. Yes, he was asleep. Then she would roll quietly away, roll again, keep rolling until she was clear of the group and it was safe to scramble to her feet.

Georgina did the first roll, the second. It was a success, she congratulated herself, rolling faster now.

Then she stopped. Someone was rolling with her. Instead of her leaving the mighty Roper behind her, he was accompanying her. The absurdity of it could have made her laugh if she had not wanted to object instead. The fool, did he think she was playing some childish game? And yet, she had to admit, it could look like a game.

His last roll had brought him within a foot of her. Their eyes looked at each other, a bare twelve inches apart.

'I—I had a cramp and wanted to get up, so I rolled here not to disturb the others,' she explained.

'Very thoughtful of you. Where is the cramp? I'll massage it.'

'No. No! It's gone now. The exercise of rolling must have fixed it.'

'As well as a strong determination,' he nodded. 'Well, if it's not there any more you may as well lie back again. There won't be anything doing until siesta's over.'

'I did think I'd scout around with the magnet.'

'This is cattle country, not mineral,' he objected.

'But there could be leads——'

'Then they'll be ignored. This is the cattle side, Brown.' Roper's lip had come out, something, Georgina had noticed, that happened when he wanted to emphasise a point.

'Yes, sir,' she said.

'Also,' went on the mighty Roper, 'I wouldn't advise any exploring, not with this mob of cattle. You heard Watson say that the beasts have been touchy.'

'They seem quiet now,' she protested.

'Don't let that silence deceive you. I've seen a rush start from the click of a cosmetic purse, the unscrewing of a lipstick. Though I hardly think ... drily ... 'you'll be doing that.'

'Of course not.'

They talked in low voices so as not to disturb the sleepers, though Roper said it would take a pack of howling dingoes to do that after lunch.

'And there aren't any of them here,' he shrugged.

'Dingoes?'

'Yes.'

'Because of the fence?' Georgina knew of the six-thousand-mile enclosure across one-third of the continent.

'Yes, our dog pen,' he nodded. 'Yet not entirely because of that, but because the dingo isn't so partial to horns and hoof as he is to sheep.'

Georgina gave a little shiver. As a man she shouldn't have, but it came instinctively. 'Poor sheep,' she said, 'to be the loser.'

'Well, such is life,' shrugged Roper, 'it's full of deceit, for man as well as sheep. Don't you agree, Brown?'

'What, sir?'

'For instance, you wouldn't think those sleeping angels there,' he nodded to the stockmen, 'could change to raw-voiced, blaspheming devils when they're called upon to keep a mob in one body, would you? Yes' ... the slightest of pauses ... 'things can be deceptive.'

Georgina said nothing.

One by one the men awakened. They conferred with Larry Roper, and Georgina gathered that they intended moving the mob.

'It's a bit sparse here,' Larry explained, coming back to Georgina, 'so they'll find another valley.'

'Are you overlanding them somewhere?'

'Heavens, no. I've been road-training the beasts for years now. No, we'll just edge them on to greener pastures until they're ready to truck. Moving a mob is a sight worth seeing, George. Get on your mount and follow up.'

Georgina went across to Ribbons and pulled herself on. Roper had untethered Gibraltar, and as he climbed up he instructed Georgina to keep well to the side in case one of the beasts got cranky. 'But,' he said, 'I think it's going to be sweet.'

It was a wonderful sight. And it remained 'sweet.' The mob, kept in order by dogs and men, moved quietly forward, a great mass of huge bodies and churning hooves. The dust after the press went by was wall-thick, and it took a long time to subside.

The cloud was still enveloping everything when the sound of a plane occurred again. It was in the distance, as before, but this time it seemed to be coming nearer and louder. Beside her, Georgina heard Roper begin to swear.

She tried to blink through the dust that still hung round, but she could see nothing. 'Is it the spy?' she asked.

'Who else? A pastoralist wouldn't do such a damn fool thing. I'll say this for most of these fellows, too, they don't come too near a mob. Why this fool is coming now is beyond me.'

'You have to expect that,' Georgina heard herself say, 'if you run two things on one property.'

His jaw tightened. 'When I want your advice I'll ask for it, Brown. Now get back.'

'Why?' Georgina was enjoying her proximity to the mob; those great rippling bodies moving past made her feel part of the earth itself.

'Just do as you're told,' he said, 'or you'll feel my crop across your back. No, I'm not joking, Brown, you've never been in a stampede. I have. Now get back.'

Georgina was hot with anger. This man was just too much, she thought. Deliberately she edged Ribbons nearer, and at the same time the craft above flew low, and the mob that had been proceeding 'sweetly' began a first beat of restless hooves.

It only took one beast to break up the quiet. It wheeled and went in the wrong direction, and at once the panic was on. Every animal seemed to turn in a different way, then they began trampling ground away from their allotted ground, ground that had not been planned.

'Get back, Brown!' Roper shouted, and at once he joined the other stockmen in fairly flying up and down the ranks. The dogs did their bit and more. The boss drover was cracking his whip over the rippling bodies of the cattle.

It was like a picture on a huge screen, Georgina thought, fascinated, not meaning to disobey Roper but so caught up with it all that she could not pull Ribbons away.

Then Ribbons backed of his own accord, backed quite violently. One of the churning beasts had caught the horse's leg, probably only superficially, but it changed Ribbons from an affable mount to a wild horse.

Not sure of what was happening, only sure that she must stick on, Georgina felt Ribbons rise on his back legs, then gallop away from the rush.

She had absolutely no control over him, and that was why she was surprised that she could hear Larry Roper's voice shouting out to her to hold on. It seemed impossible that she could follow every word he said when she couldn't even bring herself to try to check the mount.

'Hold on, Brown. He'll tire soon. Hold on, I say!'

'I can't!' she cried.

'Then break clear and I'll take you off.'

'Oh, no!' But Georgina said that to herself, and now she

did try to check Ribbons. Roper must not—*must not*—take her off.

The sudden restraint, where before his rider hadn't imposed any, took the horse by a different sort of surprise from the shock of the stampede. He halted abruptly, so abruptly that Georgina promptly flew over his head. Luckily she hit grass, coarse grass admittedly, but not gibber or rock.

She heard Ribbons whickering—he was, as Roper said, a tolerant fellow—but she heard, too, Larry's thunderous approach. In one moment, she thought dazedly, he's going to pick me up, and—and—— She took a deep steadying breath. She shut her eyes for a moment against a weaving, wreathing world, and braced herself.

Then she got up.

She stumbled, but she was on her feet again by the time Roper dismounted. He ran forward, and his eyes were two fierce blue slits.

'Top marks for quick recovery but bottom marks for disobedience, Brown,' he said, 'and that's where I'd like the marks to be. I expected you to be killed at least.'

'I'm all right,' she said unsteadily.

'Mind if I check?'

'I'm all right.' Georgina stepped back. 'I knew what I was doing, I knew I couldn't wear him out, so—so I came off.'

It was a lie, but he must have decided to accept it.

'Then top marks, as I said,' Roper drawled, 'though you could have fooled me with that fall. If you feel up to it, we'll head home now. I'll call the flying doctor and have him look you over.'

'I don't need any doctor looking me over,' she gasped.

'But I want him to. How do you think I'll feel if you sue me for damages in a month or two?'

'I won't. I'm all right, Mr Roper.' To show him Georgina crossed to Ribbons and mounted ... and it was the hardest thing she had done in her life.

'Point taken,' drawled Roper. 'You're all right,' He mounted Gibraltar, raised his whip to his cattlemen who now had the mob in full control, and they began the trek back.

Every inch of the way was a torment to Georgina, she had never felt more sick, more sad, or more sorry for herself in all her life. But she bit her lip and made herself do it, and even talked brightly as she proceeded along a track that never seemed to end.

It did end eventually, of course, and as they started through the last patch of scrub, Roper said: 'I think you should come up to the homestead.'

'No, thank you, sir.' Apart from longing to close the door on him, on everybody and everything, Georgina felt she could not have lasted any longer than the time it took to reach the hut.

'You didn't let me finish, Brown. Not for any medical attention, seeing you're so averse to it, but for a long hot bath. You seem sound in limb, but you must be bruised. I can't see you standing under the tank stand and getting any benefit there, you want something to lie in. A supply of boiling balm, or at least I find it that after a trek.'

A hot bath! Georgina felt herself yearning—even aching —to accept the offer. And why not? Baths were taken behind closed doors, or presumably they were, even here.

'Well, sir——' she said weakly.

'Good. You can strip off and lie in there for an hour. I'll even bring your meal in if it's too good to leave.'

'If you don't mind I'll just take the hot bath and then come back to bed,' she said quickly.

'They're your bruises, Brown,' Roper shrugged. 'Incidentally, I have a good medicine chest. Just shout out and I'll show you what a layman can do in the absence of a doc.'

'I'm sure you can, but I'm all right.'

'Methinks the—young man doth protest too much,' Roper drawled. 'It would be no trouble, and I'm up in medical know-how. You have to be out here.'

Wishing now she had never accepted the offer of the bath, Georgina murmured something back and they went on to the homestead.

Mrs Willmott fussed around with towels and soap, plying more than was needed.

'What a pity you're not a girl,' Roper drawled. 'I know Willy. I bet she has some bath salts stacked away somewhere.'

Georgina did not reply. There was only one thing on her mind. Had the door a key?

It was the first thing she looked for, and after she had locked herself in she gave herself up to the luxury of hot water, hot water all around her, not just applied with a sponge from a basin. She had several darkening spots that promised to turn into passable bruises, and a few scratches, but apart from these, and an exhausted feeling as though she had been put through a mangle, she had come off lightly.

She lay back and fairly wallowed. It was only when there was a tap on the door and a 'Are you drowned in there?' that she realised how long she had stayed. Regretfully she got out.

She towelled herself leisurely, looking with distaste at her crumpled pants and crushed overshirt. All at once she found herself longing for a girl's dress, pink for preference, with little buttons and a few bows ...

The shrill of a telephone broke into her thoughts.

At first she took no notice of the ring, no notice of Mrs Willmott answering. Then, insidiously, as though she could not escape it, she listened.

'Yes?' said Mrs Willmott.

After that: 'Yes, they are here.'

Next: 'No, I'm afraid I couldn't at the moment, it's been a field day today and the bath was the first order— No, there's no connection to the bathroom.' (That was accompanied by Mrs Willmott's snort.)

'Yes, that can be done. Your number, miss?'—Miss,

trembled Georgina.

'The message will be passed on,' Georgina heard Mrs Willmott say. 'Good day.'

The phone went down and with its descent came Mrs Willmott's: 'Are you out yet, George?'

Georgina came into the hall.

The first thing she noticed was that Larry Roper was stretched in an easy chair within easy listening distance of the phone; the second thing was that he was looking at her closely. So he had learned something! He would have been near enough to the connection to hear every word.

But it seemed it was not that, or if it was he didn't say so. Instead he drawled: 'You do clean up well, George, you look a different colour.'

Above his head was a wall mirror, and Georgina saw herself in it, scrubbed and pink and not at all as she wanted to be in the presence of this man.

'If we'd known you were finished, George, you could have taken your call yourself.' It was Mrs Willmott. Roper was still estimating her.

'A call for me?' she asked.

'From a young lady,' Mrs Willmott smiled archly. 'She said she was your stepsister. Now that's a change from a cousin, I thought.' A laugh.

'She is a stepsister,' Georgina said bleakly. What had Joanne had to say?

Then it came to Georgina that Mrs Willmott was still calling her George, so evidently Joanne had not asked for her by name.

'Are you sure *I* was wanted?' she dared.

'Oh, yes, quite sure. "Is George there?" she said.'

'Yes,' Georgina agreed, for she could see it all now, or at least she could piece together what Mrs Willmott had heard, and that had been Joanne emphasising the name that she had given her stepsister in derision. 'You're George, not Georgina,' she had flung at her.

It had evidently deceived Mrs Willmott, but what of the

mighty Roper, lounging back in his chair now and listening to it all, wearing that faintly derisive, contemptuous face he frequently put on?

'She'll ring again,' said Mrs Willmott. 'Unless,' arch again, 'you want to ring her first.'

'No.'

'That's the way, George,' came in Larry Roper idly, 'play hard to get. All females have only one thing in mind really, and that's that plain gold ring. I give her five minutes to ring you.'

'Then I won't be here.' But even as she said it, Georgina knew she would *have* to be here. So far Joanne had ruined nothing, but if she was put off a second time ...

'Any bruises?' Roper asked without much interest, evidently bored with the phone topic.

'A few.'

'Strategic places?' He yawned.

That, thought Georgina icily, means what you call strategic places.

'I'll mend,' she evaded.

'Make sure of that.' He was getting up. With luck he would be out of earshot by the time Joanne rang again. She could manage Mrs Willmott but not him.

At that moment the phone shivered, then began to shrill again. This time Roper leaned over and answered it.

'Yes, Roper's. Yes, right here.'

He turned and handed the receiver to Georgina. 'It's for you again, George.'

Georgina took up and cradled it, then she looked at him significantly and waited. He did not move. After all, why should he? It was his house.

'Go ahead, George,' he prompted blandly.

Wretchedly Georgina obeyed.

'Yes?' she gulped.

CHAPTER EIGHT

'Is that George?' Joanne's voice came coolly, distinctively and with significance on the *George*, over the wire.

'Yes. Is it Joanne?' Georgina asked shakily.

'Of course. Who else? What tricks are you up to now, George?'

'No tricks. I came on here from Windmill Junction.'

'Yes, I've discovered that, but I had to go to that god-forsaken hole to find out. When I heard nothing from you I rang Windmill, and when that store bumpkin told me you'd moved on but he didn't know where, I went up and put the question a little more strongly to him.'

'But Bill didn't know where,' Georgina protested.

'He did by the time I put him through a few hoops. He remembered sending a letter for you. He said it was just after a——'

'Yes,' Georgina came in quickly before Joanne could finish, after an unsuccessful phone call.

'So I put two and two together and knew it had to be there. I knew you had no other contacts. Well, enough of how and where—what's more like it, when?'

'When?'

'Yes, when. There's a little matter of some money owing to me, George, and running away isn't going to get you out of it.'

'Joanne, the last thing I intended was to cheat you!'

'I must say it didn't look like that when you exchanged the caravan for a bag of groceries.'

'Bill tuckered me, and the van wouldn't sell, Joanne,' Georgina said firmly.

'But the other things—say a manuscript and a type-writer?'

'I can explain all that.'

'You'd better pay, not explain, George.'

'I will, Joanne, I'll be sending you a postal order.'

'It had better be soon. Very soon. I'm needing that money. Why'—curiosity in Joanne's voice now—'did you choose to go out there?'

'To avoid going back to Sydney.'

'But why *there*, particularly? I suspect you, George, you've always had schemes in your head. What's so attractive up there?'

'Just the things I like,' said Georgina, 'you know how I love the inland.'

'Humph! All right then, the cash, George, otherwise I'm coming after it. That, and to find out how a feller like you ticks. Incidentally, I'm beginning on the money side immediately by reversing my charges to you on this call. See you, George.'

Joanne's receiver went firmly down. Georgina put her own receiver back more slowly.

'I'll go now, Mr Roper,' she said.

'Not so fast,' he detained her.

'You mean the reverse charges? Joanne said she was doing that. I'll pay for them, of course.'

'Of course, but still not so fast. I think you should stop for a bite, Brown. One way and another it's been quite a day for you, hasn't it?' His face softened. 'I don't think you'd feed yourself properly if you went back.'

'I would, sir. Anyway, what I most want to do is go to bed.'

'You can do that here. Willy will love it. And there's always a spare pair of pyjama pants.'

Georgina swallowed at the pants but kept her face immobile, or she tried to. 'I would prefer to go to the hut,' she said.

He shrugged. 'Oh, very well, Brown. I'll have one of the

men drive you down. I'm too tuckered myself.'

'A walk would take some of the stiffness off me, do me good,' Georgina offered.

'Have it your own way. You appear to be doing that, anyhow, by that conversation just now. I had to hear it. *Do* you owe money?'

'No. I mean—— well—yes.'

'Which?' he insisted.

'Which?'

'You do owe money or you don't owe money? Yes? No?'

'Yes,' Georgina said miserably.

'Always pay your debts, George.'

'Yes, sir.'

'Also while you are employed by me, obey orders. I haven't spoken about that performance of yours today, I thought you'd had enough. But anything you're suffering now is entirely your own fault. When I told you to move back I meant move back. Except that I didn't have time to administer it, I would have seen that you did it.'

'Administer what?' she asked.

'What you've obviously never had and should have. You look incredulous, but I assure you I still would have, *and* in front of the men. Indeed, if I hadn't, they would have themselves. They couldn't afford not to. You don't play around with a mob, it's like playing with death. Yes, Willy?' The housekeeper had come in.

'I thought if George wouldn't stay that at least he'd take this hamper.' Mrs Willmott put down a laden bag beside Georgina.

'Thank you,' Georgina said, not far from tears. She wondered what the mighty Roper would say if he found a fat droplet trickling down her cheek.

'With a bag like that you'll have to be taken,' Roper was sighing resignedly. 'I'll do it.'

'But——' she protested.

'Get out and get in and shut up,' he advised.

Georgina did just that.

To her surprise, for she had expected more questioning, Roper dropped her at the hut and at once turned the car back to the homestead. Relieved, Georgina shut the door behind her, and was in bed in an incredibly short time. She slept at once, and she slept well into the next morning. At last she woke up, rose, splashed water on her face, got into fresh jeans and clean loose shirt and brewed coffee.

She was on the second cup when Roper knocked on the door. She could see no car and no horse, and, following her glance, he told her he had walked. All geologists, he reminded her, have to know how to walk.

'What do you want me to do today, Mr Roper?' Georgina asked docilely.

'Nothing, you can catch up with your study. I told you that you would have spare time in the ad. Yes, get on with that thesis. Iain Sutherland, isn't it?'

'Yes, sir.'

'I'll probably not need you for several weeks, Brown. As a matter of fact I'll be away for that length of time myself. Now, about that phone call last night.'

'Yes, Mr Roper. I must pay you.'—Out of what? Georgina thought bleakly, for there was very little in her purse.

'It will be deducted from your salary. On that money subject, I gathered from the conversation that the young lady——'

'My stepsister.'

His eyes glinted. 'If you say so ... is waiting for a remittance from you.'

'Yes,' she nodded.

'You are aware, I trust, Brown, that you won't be paid for a month yet?'

'A month——?' Her voice failed her.

'Yes, a month. It's the practice on these stations to hold on to a month's salary both to safeguard the employer and benefit the employee.'

'I—I don't think she'll wait that long.'

'Your stepsister?' he demanded.

'Yes.'

'I see.'

There was silence for a while.

'What did you do to her to make her so antagonistic?' the man asked presently. 'Come clean, Brown, you can open up and talk to me, it's between men.'

'Nothing,' she muttered.

'Nothing. Well' ... humorously ... 'I expect that's as good an answer as any.'

'Sir?'

'Pretty, is she?' he asked.

'Very.'

'And wasted on you.'

'Sir, she *is* my stepsister.'

'Stick to your story, Brown,' Roper smiled, 'but don't try to stop me seeing her side to all this.'

'What do you mean?' asked Georgina.

'There's no greater wrath than a woman spurned. I think the right word is fury, not wrath, but you get the idea. I think, too, we'll have to put all this to rights, Brown, and pay the girl up here. *You* may not appreciate her, but I can assure you a lot of our female-hungry men will.'

'Including yourself?'—Now why had she said that?

He shrugged. 'Could happen. I've been out of circulation long enough, I believe, so I may emerge from my shell and mingle again. Tell me what you think, Brown. Do you think I'd have any appeal? To this—stepsister, I mean? No, don't answer without giving it fair thought. *Look* at me, Brown. Really look at me.—Well, what do you think?'

'I don't think,' she said numbly.

'You don't think I'd appeal to her?'

'No ... I mean ...'

'Too rough, perhaps, too raw and crude, she'd prefer your more genteel and gentle type?' His voice hardened.

'But she doesn't. You heard her.' Georgina knew she was getting into dangerous waters.

'Yes, I heard her.' His voice was dry, and Georgina would have liked to have looked up at him again, tried to pick his thoughts, but she didn't dare.

He was taking something from his pocket. It was a wallet, and he was flicking out some notes.

'For this time only,' he said, and pushed them across.

'This is too much!'

'You don't have to send it all,' he pointed out.

'I mean it's too much wages.'

'It's the set man's rate,' he informed her. He closed the wallet and put it back in his pocket.

'Thank you, Mr Roper,' she said in a small voice.

He shrugged that away, but still did not leave, although he had said it was her free day.

'Mrs Willmott is worried about you, George,' he said abruptly.

'I'm all right,' she answered, 'I was a bit exhausted yesterday, but I'm all right now.'

'She's worried about you in a different way; she's worried that you're becoming what I am, at least what I was, for I've decided to pull out of it and take up life once more.'

'Sir?' she looked inquiringly at him.

'I'm talking about women,' Roper said coolly. 'Wine and song with them if you like, but women. You certainly shrink away when there's a prospect of women, don't you, George?'

Actually, thought Georgina, I shrink away when the prospect is men.

'Mrs Willmott gathered all this,' Roper continued, 'when you showed such distaste for speaking to the young lady over the phone.'

'Joanne is my——'

'Yes, you've told us that. Well, son, Willy doesn't like it, and when Mrs Wilmott doesn't like something she sets about fixing it.'

'Fixing——?' she faltered.

'We're having a party, a barn-dance, as soon as I get

96

back, Brown. There are some very pretty girls up top, and one of them must be your type.'

At last the big man did rise.

'I'll see you when I return,' he nodded, and went out.

After he had gone Georgina sat for a long, long time. A party with girls, she was thinking. Girls whom you were expected to talk with, compliment, ask to dance! Well, that brought a definite full stop to everything, she knew, that meant the absolute end. She couldn't pretend, not in a thing like that. However, she wasn't going to worry about it yet—she would be gone before Larry Roper returned and the party was put on. With the big boss away it would be easy to leave. She would simply bike up to the Brydens'— Craig should be on his rounds again quite soon and be able to take her back to Sydney—and that would close the chapter of Roper's.

Only ... and Georgina squeezed out another cup of coffee from the pot and drank it cold without even noticing ... she didn't want the chapter closed. This was her country and she hated to go. There was something else, another reason, but Georgina refused even to consider that.

She decided to wait a while before she finally took off. Roper had said he would be gone for a few weeks, so she would be quite safe. Also she did not know the Brydens; they might be Craig's lessees, but that did not mean they had to be cordial to her. Quite feasibly they could resent her—tenants usually disliked their landlords and a friend of the landlord could be equally unpopular. Georgina decided to leave her escape once more until the day before Roper's return. Only this time she *meant* to escape.

Meanwhile she got through some work on the book and some work for the boss. She sent away a postal order to Joanne, promising to send more when she had earned it. She gave Joanne an account of the place guaranteed, she thought, to put Joanne right off. No diversions here, she told her stepsister. Nothing to look at, no life at all. Just scenery. (Joanne was indifferent to scenery, especially the

97

western variety.) Most of all and a fact that should influence Joanne, there were no men. The last was not true, yet in her own case these days she might have been speaking the truth. For after Larry Roper had left Georgina had not seen a man until she went up the second week for some supplies. Then she saw a crowd of them.

'You should have been up before, George, the bread must have been uneatable,' grumbled Willy. 'Besides, we needed you. We need all our hands. I was just about to send down for you.'

'What's happened, Mrs Willmott?'

'It's what's going to happen. The party, of course. Mr Roper said he intended to speak about it to you.' Mrs Willmott looked archly at Georgina and Georgina tried not to understand what she was being arch about and not to flush. *A girl for George.* It was written very plainly in Willy's kind brown eyes.

'It all takes a lot of preparation,' went on Mrs Willmott, 'it's not like just opening up your house to guests. The house is always ready, but a barn isn't. A barn has to be emptied, cleaned up and decorated. Now there' ... with a beam ... 'is where you can come in.'

'Me?'

Mrs Willmott looked uncomfortable. 'Forgive me for saying it, George, but you're not—well, quite like the others. You're more the—well, the artistic type. Their idea of decoration, the men's, is some streamers and balloons, and there they stop. But I think you could do it beautifully, George.'

'When is the party?' Georgina asked.

'Saturday.'

'Is Mr Roper coming?'

'Unfortunately he'll miss it, he won't be home until the following week.'

'I see.'

'Please, George,' appealed Mrs Willmott, 'do add an artistic touch. I know you'd sooner Mr Roper saw what you

98

can do, that's only natural, but I'm sure he would be pleased when we told him all about it. We could even leave the decorations up for him to see. And think, George, how proud you'll be when all the girls admire the effect. You'll be—— oh, dear!' Mrs Willmott giggled. 'I was almost going to say the belle of the ball,' she confessed. 'You'll be the *beau*, George. Every girl will be clamouring to dance with you.'

'And Mr Roper won't be here?' Georgina persisted.

'Unfortunately no,' Mrs Willmott said regretfully a second time, 'but that won't worry the girls,' she added brightly, 'not with a young man around. You must know how young things are, being young yourself.'

'And he won't be back?'

'No.' It was quite definite.

'I'll do it, Mrs Willmott,' Georgina said. Why not? she thought. Why not make this my final contribution to Roper's, my swan song, and do a really good job, for I know I can. Also, she thought, I have no fears now about the party night. Where I wouldn't have been able to face up to Larry Roper and say No, I won't go, I could face up to Mrs Willmott and the men—say I simply won't be coming. Say I have a fever, a sprained ankle, anything but the truth. The truth that as soon as I've decorated the barn for the dance, and the dance is on, noisily on, I'll be leaving Roper's before Roper returns. *This time for sure.*

'Yes, I'll do it, Mrs Willmott,' she said again.

'Thank you, George.' The woman smiled.

Georgina really enjoyed herself fixing the barn for the party, and she knew it progressed well, for the men praised it lavishly every time they passed.

'Had you been a stockie,' Mrs Willmott said once, 'they would have tagged you Georgina for making it pretty like this.' She giggled. 'They're a rough, tough, goodhearted lot, but they can be outspoken. But you being a geologist, George, they put you in a different category, they respect your brain and don't look for brawn or muscle.'

Just as well, thought Georgina.

Nothing was a trouble to her; she hung the streamers, paper lanterns and balloons that the men seemed to think were necessary because a party wasn't a party without them, but she went out on the bike as well and found a lot of things you didn't expect to find in this nowhere land. Trailing vines ... no one knew their names, so she called them flood vines, just like Craig's flood flowers ... some native ti, armfuls of desert daisies and Salvation Jane. She even went as far as the gibber and looked for suitable stones, round smooth stones with a warm colouring. These she placed at the base of a contrived waterfall that she persuaded the station electrician to fix up, so that at a press of a button the water would splash down. She had put red paper round all the electric globes to add a pink glamour, but round the 'waterfall' she put a greenish blue. The effect was wonderful. Even Georgina herself had to stand and admire.

The night before the party she packed all her things, just as she had previously. For the first time she recalled the note to Larry Roper that had blown away. She hadn't thought of it since. This time, she told herself, she would fasten it on.

She did not sit on the doorstep that night and say goodbye to her beloved west—she refused to permit nostalgia. She had to go and that was that. It was out of her hands. She might not have this opportunity again, with all the station hands over at the barn and no one to see her leave, to stop her.

She put the finishing touches to the barn on Saturday morning. She 'dewed' the flowers from a watering can and tried the waterfall to make sure it played. Finally she looked around her with satisfaction.

But just as it always is, there was a flaw. One of the big balloons, and it *would* be a prominent one, had decided to deflate. Sighing, Georgina fetched the big ladder and climbed up to inflate the balloon again.

She was fastening it back when she felt eyes on her. It was a feeling, she thought, not just a sense of someone watching. She did not let the scrutiny put her out, for she was very high and had to use caution; she finished the fastening, then looked down.

'Oh, no!' She was so dismayed she said it aloud.

It was Roper.

He was standing at the barn door and he was regarding the scene ... and her. That his face clearly showed his approval might have pleased Georgina if she had not thought at once:

'Now how do I get out of a party ... a party with girls ... one of them supposedly my type?'

She began to descend, and because he was still watching she tried to make it jaunty, as a young athletic man would descend not a mere cautious girl. Two rungs down she slipped, but she righted herself at once. But the near-accident had alerted Larry Roper, and he ran forward—right into a screen that Georgina had concealed a little too subtly with vines.

The next minute he and the screen were on the floor.

It made enough row to bring Mrs Willmott and a few of the men to the scene. While they fussed, spoke of possible concussion and finally decided to carry the boss to bed, Georgina resumed her cautious descent once more. But once down, she sought out Mrs Willmott and found her in the homestead ringing up for the Flying Doctor. Mrs Willmott never took chances.

'He might only be winded, Mrs Willmott,' Georgina said.

'Perhaps, but we can't take the risk. Go into Mr Roper's bedroom and send the men out, George; they mean well, but they're clumsy big brutes and talk too loudly. You're gentler—oh' ... an afterthought ... 'undress him, George.'

Georgina, who had turned to do what Mrs Willmott had asked, stopped short.

'Do—what?' she blurted.

'Undress him. Get him into his pyjamas, poor dear, ready for the doctor.'

'Yes,' said Georgina, 'I thought that was what you said.'

She went along the corridor to what was evidently the boss's room; a brown and tan room, apart from rows of books quite bare, even monkish. She said, and she hoped her voice didn't tremble: 'I'll take over if you like.'

The men did like. Sickrooms were not their forte. They left at once, and as soon as they reached the door Georgina could hear them thankfully lighting up. She turned and looked at the patient.

He was very pale and a lump was growing out of his temple even as she gazed at him.

'Doctor's coming, George,' called Mrs Willmott from the hall. 'Have you settled him yet?'

'No,' she said.

'Then do it, George. Or is he too heavy? Shall I help you, or perhaps call one of the men?'

'No,' said Georgina a second time, thinking that if anything could be worse, then that would be worse. She began unbuttoning his shirt.

He was a heavyweight, but as he was beyond resistance she got the shirt successfully off. Like all the men up here he wore either shirt or singlet, never both. Shirt off, the mighty Roper lay bare-chested. She looked around for pyjamas. She found the trousers and was searching for the jacket when he said very distinctly from his pillows: 'I only wear one half.'

Georgina jumped. It was the last thing she had expected. So he wasn't 'out' as she had thought! She picked the pants up and crossed to him.

'The doctor's on his way,' she said.

He nodded.

'Perhaps—perhaps you can put these on.' She held them out to him, but he did not take them.

'The cord,' he said expressionlessly, 'ties in the front.'

'Of course.' She turned the garment round, and there

was a moment's silence.

'Tell Willy to make me a cup of tea,' Roper groaned, 'my head's giving me hell. I could do with a stiff drink, but if the doctor's coming——'

'Yes.' Georgina hurried out at once.

She brought the tea back the moment Mrs Willmott made it, but did not give it to him. The man appeared to have fallen asleep. Perhaps while he was asleep she could—yes, perhaps she could——

'Not to worry.' His eyes were still closed, but he must have seen her through those blue slits of his, 'I've already changed into the appropriate pants.'

'You've——' her voice faltered.

'If you don't believe me, look. Anyway, there's all my outdoor clobber on the floor to prove it.' There was, she saw.

'You shouldn't have,' she protested weakly.

'All the same you're glad I did, aren't you, George?' The slits were wider now. 'I can see we'll have to have a talk together, Brown. You can't expect to stay on an outback station and not face up to a few home truths. Like always bathing in a basin, for example. How do I know that, George? Because the damn tank's shower connection has been turned off since before you came, and it's still turned off, yet you always look well scrubbed. Like——'

But Larry Roper never finished. Whatever had happened to him when he fell now caught up with him at full strength. He gave a little moan and lost consciousness.

'Mrs Willmott!' called Georgina in concern.

But she also called in vast relief.

CHAPTER NINE

NOT long afterwards Georgina heard the whirr of a small craft over the homestead, but at once the sound diminished.

'The doctor will be looking for an airstrip,' explained Mrs Willmott, who had come in at Georgina's call and now watched their patient from the other side of the bed.

Georgina knew by this time that it was not always the same strip, because when Roper had surprised her by arriving too early that first time, he had landed his craft further north on a neighbouring property. That it had been his enemy's property had not mattered since only the Brydens and not Craig had been there, so the mighty Roper had been able to avail himself without any unpleasant encounter.

'The men have marked one of our southern paddocks for the doctor,' Mrs Willmott went on. 'It only had a few beasts grazing and it didn't take long to move them out.'

'Marked?' Windmill Junction had had no strip at all, you had had to travel overland from another field to get to it, so Georgina was puzzled by this. Did they paint guide lines, the way lanes were painted on roads?

'They mark it with upturned white plastic buckets,' said Mrs Willmott, 'it's the quickest way. There's a car going out for the doctor now.'

Within five minutes the Flying Doctor was coming through the door, a young man with the deep-set eyes of one who frequently looks into distance. He greeted: 'Hullo, Willy,' and gave Georgina a friendly salute.

'Mr Larry's geo,' Mrs Willmott introduced, and Georgina, modestly about to deny this rank, saw that it didn't matter anyway, and just nodded back to the doctor instead.

'What have we here?' said the doctor, looking down at the sickbed. 'First time I've ever been called to the mighty Roper.' He leaned over the patient.

'He means Mr Roper,' explained Mrs Willmott unnecessarily to Georgina. She added: 'Mr Larry's got on so well both with what his father left him and what he's made for himself that he's right at the top now. "Mighty Roper" isn't meant to be—well——'

'Derogatory?' helped Georgina.

'Yes. It isn't meant like that at all. Is he concussed, Doctor?'

The doctor nodded. 'Yes, but he's coming out of it. Slowly, but he's on the way back.'

'Will you take him to the Base with you?'

'No. Although I'm not actually concerned about him, I might be if I were rash enough to move him at this juncture. If he stays here, and by that I mean if he's kept from riding around and doing the hundred and one things he always does—in short if he stays put as he is now—he'll be all right.'

'For how long?' Mrs Willmott asked.

'A day and a night should do the trick. Even half of that, knowing Roper, will help.'

'Too late,' Mrs Willmott sighed, then, seeing the doctor's surprised face, she explained herself.

'The party's on tonight, the barn-dance. He won't be able to go?'

'He most certainly won't. I won't be denying him much, but I decidedly won't be recommending dancing. Just give him a look-in now and then, then if either of you can be spared to sit beside him, that would help. I'll leave a sedative, but it's not all that important. I know Larry, he's as strong as one of his bulls.' He grinned, then looked persuasively at Mrs Willmott.

'Do you still make those pumpkin scones?'

'Of course. You can watch Mr Larry, can't you, George?'

Georgina said she could, and when they had gone she found herself a chair and drew it up by the side of the bed.

The colour was stealing back into Roper's cheeks. Very slowly, as the doctor had said, he was on his way back to consciousness.

Across at the barn she could hear a piano being moved in; she knew it was a piano because every now and then an onlooker decided to press a key. It seemed as though the festive arrangements were still proceeding, and Georgina wondered whether this was because it was too late to cancel them or because out here a party was a party and only flood, fire or famine could intervene.

She heard the doctor leave in the car for his plane again, and later the throb of the plane engine as he left for the Base. Mrs Willmott came in soon after with a cup of tea for her.

'He's looking better, George.' Willy stood regarding Roper.

'Yes,' Georgina said woodenly.

'As soon as he gets his senses he'll be wanting to get up. I know Mr Larry.'

'But the doctor said——'

'Exactly. And I depend on you, George, to make Mr Larry see sense. do as he's told. Poor boy'—now she was looking at Georgina instead of Roper—'you've worked hard with those decorations, it's too hard for you to be deprived like this.'

'Deprived?' asked Georgina gladly, for this was wonderful. Now she need make no excuses about tonight, tell no lies; it seemed she was simply expected *not* to be there.

'Yes, George. I'm afraid it will have to be you who's left to watch him. Bedrooms are definitely not the place for cattlemen. Talk about bulls in china shops! Then I,' apologetically, 'have to manage the supper.'

Georgina smiled. 'Mrs Willmott, I don't mind, I assure you.'

'You know I don't think you do, George, you're a kind lad. We must have another barn-dance and it must be especially for you, George; I do want you to begin to mingle. Oh, Mr Roper is coming round nicely. I'm sure I saw one eyelid flick just then. Finished your tea, George? Then I'll take out the cup.'

For another ten minutes Georgina sat on. If Mrs Willmott had been right about the eyelid-flicking, she did not see it. Yet every time she turned away, to change her position or to glance through the window, to take up a book, put it down—she was sharply aware that something had moved. An eyelid?

Mrs Willmott brought in a tray of dinner, and later she took the depleted dishes out again. Over in the barn a violin began to tune up. Shadows crept over the windowsill, but they were soon pushed out by the lights of cars, jeeps, waggons and trucks. The partygoers were arriving.

Mrs Willmott came in again, in blue crêpe covered with a large apron.

'Poor George! I suppose I should say poor Mr Roper, too, but what you don't know about you can't miss, can you, and he appears not to know. Yes, he's taking his time coming round all right, almost as if he intended it, and yet he looks quite healthy and pink.'

Georgina considered the mighty Roper looked healthy, but not pink; more a leather brown. But she did agree secretly that Roper looked as though he were doing things to his own design, not anyone else's, which after all would be typical of the man.

'I'll go then, George,' said Mrs Willmott. 'If you don't see me for a spell you'll know I'm run off my feet.' Her cheerful voice betrayed her satisfaction at being so necessary as she went out.

Georgina sat on, and presently the last light of the last arrival flashed off and the room's darkness was undisturbed again.

'Hullo, Brown,' Larry Roper said.

'Oh!' Georgina had not expected this, and she started. She pretended she had not jumped by saying practically:

'So you're with us again.'

'How hospital-like you sound, Brown.' He made a face in the dark, she could just see it. ' "So you're with us again". Why don't you add: "How are we now? Did we have a good rest? Are we going to try very hard to get well? Are we going to eat our tea?" '

'I'm sorry, sir.'

He looked rueful. 'No, *I* am sorry. I was only teasing, of course. I suppose you were expecting the orthodox recovery. A slow flickering of the eyelids then a confused: "Where am I? Who are you?" '

'Well, yes,' Georgina half-laughed.

'But I know where I am and who you are. In fact I've been listening for the last hour. For instance, I know the party's on but that you're not going—instead you're nursing me.'

'Watching you,' Georgina corrected.

'A pity.'

'A pity that I'm watching and not nursing? But the doctor didn't seem to think you needed a nurse. Anyway, I'm not a nurse. I mean' ... hastily ... 'a male nurse.'

'No, you're not.' A pause. 'But I really meant it was a pity you weren't in the barn.'

'Why, sir?' she asked.

'Why? Because there's nothing, just nothing like a barn party ... unless, of course, it's a barn wedding.' His eyes gleamed.

'That's something I wouldn't have thought would interest you, Mr Roper.'

'No? But I think I told you I was considering coming out of the shell again.'

'Interesting,' Georgina murmured. 'What caused the desire to return to life?'

'You, as a matter of fact,' he said calmly.

'Me!' For a moment Georgina's heart lurched. Surely

he didn't ... surely he hadn't ...

He cut in at once, and suavely. He said: 'Mrs Willmott's chatter about bringing you out of yourself took me back to my own green years. I envied you your youth, so I decided to do something about it for myself before I was left behind.'

'Oh,' said Georgina with relief. For a few moments she had thought he had seen Georgina in her, not George.

Across from the barn wafted the opening waltz. Only a piano, a fiddle and an accordion, but the night lent a magic to the music and the notes crept in almost unbearably sweet.

Out here, thought Georgina, the music would always be yesterday's, as this music was now; there were too many intervening miles for latest hits. But Irving Berlin's *Always* fitted her mood perfectly. She followed the words with quiet lips. 'I'll be loving you always.' She wondered what Larry would say if she told him that that was why she was here now, why she was living a lie, that it was because she loved this inland so much and so completely, that she must now love it for ever. For always.

'Mr Roper——' she said spontaneously.

'Yes, George?' he mocked her tone.

'Are you comfortable?' Georgina said instead.

About midnight the party broke up. It was early by city standards, but every car, jeep, waggon and truck had miles to travel home.

Mrs Willmott tiptoed in, flushed, triumphant, regretful and dog-tired all at the same time.

'How is he, George?'

'Quite good. We talked for a while, but I think he's gone off now.' He hadn't spoken for an hour, but then neither had she. The music had weaved between them and there had been no need for words.

'That's splendid, George. Now you go to bed, boy. No, not down at the hut, here in the homestead. It's my turn to watch.'

'No, Mrs Willmott,' she protested.

'But, George, I'd like you in the house in case.'

'I meant I'm not leaving the room. I'm staying. Yes, I mean that, Mrs Willmott. You've been run off your feet—in your own words—and I've only been sitting here.'

It took a little persuasion, but Georgina could see the longing for rest in Mrs Willmott's face. She renewed her efforts, and presently the housekeeper said: 'For an hour only, then, just to give my legs a rest.'

She brought Georgina more tea, gave Roper an estimating look and agreed that he seemed fine, told Georgina to call her, then went out wearily.

Georgina closed the door after her and came back to the chair. She saw the lights of the barn go off, then the lights of the mess. She listened and heard Roper's steady breathing, and after a watching hour she slumped in the chair and drifted to sleep herself.

She awoke to the first lemon-grey rays of morning and to a man's bright blue eyes. The man was on the bed but not in the bed; he was sitting on it. He was also fully dressed.

As Georgina blinked at him he said: 'Sugar, Brown?' and she saw that he had brought in a tray.

'This is terrible!' Georgina was annoyed with herself. 'I'm left to watch you and you've been watching me.'

'On the contrary, I only gave you a quick glance, then I got myself up and went out to make a cuppa. Oh no, Brown, why should I want to look at a young feller?' A pause. 'I asked you about sugar.'

She flushed. 'One, thanks. How do you feel?'

'Completely recovered.'

'Yet the Flying Doctor said——'

'Yes, I know, but the doctor's not infallible. I'm back to where I was, so I go on as I would have. Doesn't that make sense?'

'Perhaps, but——'

'So what I intended to do and planned to do, is what I'll do now. I have a few loose ends to attend to—you always have ends when you've been away for a while. That will take me up to Wednesday, after which you and I leave on a safari.'

'A what?' she gasped.

'An expedition ... exploration ... call it what you will. In short, we're on the hunt. We're taking rations and sleeping bags and head for—well, I'll give you the latitudes and longitudes when we're on the track, though incidentally it won't be a track.'

'It won't?' Georgina asked feebly.

'Where we'll be going, probably no man has been before.'

'You mean it will be beyond Roper's?'

'Of course,' Roper said impatiently. 'We're after the big stuff now, Brown, not just the stuff we know is here in our backyard, but the stuff not enclosed within boundary fences, even fences the size of Roper's. Well'—glaring at Georgina —'you might show some enthusiasm, man.'

She was dismayed. 'Oh, I want to see it, of course, but——'

'Yes, Brown?'

'But—my work here?'

'You mean your studies?' he demanded.

'No, I can do those on the way. I really meant my work for you.'

'Stupid boy, this work will be for me. We'll be looking, George, only the looking will be much more intense than it ever was before.' He studied her. 'Have you been on a safari?'

'Only in a caravan,' she confessed.

'This one will be in a four-wheel drive jeep and no caravan, no cover, not even a groundsheet. We'll need every inch of space for tools.'

'Yes, sir.' Georgina said it slowly, and at once he set his eyes on her.

'You sound only half-hearted, and half-heartedness is something I haven't found in you before. Look, George, you'd better hit the hay and we'll talk about it later.'

'Yes, sir,' she repeated.

Roper was at the window now, looking out at the morning that with every second was gathering gold and losing grey.

'Bit of a difference, isn't it?' he mused.

'A difference? Oh, you mean the difference between night and day.'

'No, I meant a difference between a safari out there' ... he pointed ... 'to music and paper roses in here last night.' A pause. ' "I'll be loving you" was what they were playing, wasn't it, Brown?'

'I'm not up in songs, Mr Roper.'

'*Wasn't it*, Brown?' he insisted.

'Well—yes.'

He nodded. 'I've always liked that thing. Called *Always*, isn't it? You know I'm all for always. Are you?'

'What, sir?' she said, bewildered.

'Oh, for heaven's sake, Brown, get out and put your head down. I'll contact you later.'

'Yes, Mr Roper.'

Georgina went out of the room, out of the homestead and down the track to the hut. There she put her head down as directed and closed her eyes, but it was a long time before sleep came in spite of her weariness. *Always*, she was hearing the Mighty Roper saying, *I'm all for always. Are you?*

Yes, Mr Roper, I am, Georgina could have answered. For instance I want to be here always, I want——

Suddenly Georgina was sitting up in the narrow bed. Oh, no, I don't, she protested. I can't! I won't! and yet—and yet——

I do.

At daylight a few mornings later the jeep pulled up. Roper did not get out, he only blew the horn, something he could do here because there was no one else to hear. Georgina came out of the hut and went across to him.

'What do I bring?' she asked.

'Nothing.'

'Nothing? But——'

He frowned. 'You'll be living in the clothes you wear, Brown, and if that offends you, then you can find a wurlie and wash them, and go around as nature intended you to go until they dry.'

'Oh, I'm not complaining, sir, I just wanted to know,' Georgina said hastily. These present clothes, she knew, were going to last the distance, however long.

'All I've allowed us is a billy, a frying pan, two mugs, two plates and two sleeping bags,' went on Roper. 'I would have halved that, except I didn't know how you'd feel about sharing my plate, but I knew I wouldn't like sharing your bag. Now if you were only Georgia, not George——' he grinned.

'Georgina,' Georgina said automatically.

'Come again?' He looked across at her.

'Generally the female version of George is Georgina. I mean it's a more usual form.'

'Is it now?' He was still looking at her.

Georgina got in to the jeep, an almost empty jeep now, but it would be a different story when they came back with their rock samples. They set off.

It was wonderful to be able to plunge into the scrub and not worry about the absence of any road. The four-wheel drive permitted this, and the flat terrain, though it challenged them often with its sudden ditches, its sudden magnetic anthills and its sudden rock outcrops, never actually halted them, only demanded that they detour. And such confusing detours they were that often they seemed to go round in circles.

'I don't know how you can find your way,' said Georgina at last.

'I wouldn't think of trying it without my friend.' Roper nodded to a compass hooked on the control panel. 'We are now——' He consulted it and gave Georgina the bearing.

Around noon Georgina glimpsed blackbutt trees and drew Roper's attention to them. They went cross-country to the blackbutt stand, finding nearby gossan in the form of light brown silica.

'Got your magnet, Brown?' Roper asked.

'Yes, sir.' Georgina withdrew it, and at once felt a pull.

She looked excitedly up at Roper, but he did not respond to her find at once: he stood looking at her instead. Her cheeks, had she known it, were carnation pink and her tan eyes danced.

'Anyone ever tell you you'd make a pretty girl, George?' There was an odd note in his voice.

Georgina dropped the magnet and turned away. She heard him pick it up, give a grunt of satisfaction at the same reaction that she had felt, then she heard him say:

'Sorry, George, and all that. You can't help how you look any more than I can help the way I express myself.'

'But that *can* be helped, Mr Roper.' Georgina was still annoyed.

'And your looks can't?' he interpreted. 'No, I didn't say that, boy, it just slipped out. Forget it, George. How about nosh?'

Georgina prepared the meal, and she tried to do it as a man might, without any small detail.

They ate sitting on the ground. It was very dry here. That was the way of the Wet; some corners were inundated, some were almost parched.

'Did you bring much water?' Georgina asked. She had noticed that the demijohn she had used for the billy was not very deep.

'Only that.' He nodded to the container. 'I know all the holes around, and I also know my survival procedure. Finally I know how to rob an upside-down river.'

'A what?'

'Australian Inside rivers flow underneath the ground, not on top as respectable streams do. It's crazy land out here, magic but crazy. After a Wet has gone, even in a dry part like this you needn't parch. Look.' He had taken up a stick and he pushed it in the ground, then withdrew it. It was dry.

114

He probed again, deeper. The stick came out wet.

'There's water there,' he said.

There were so many geological signs around them they did not leave there, in fact only the setting sun and the advisability of eating while they could still see halted their explorations.

They boiled up another billy, ate more brisket on homestead bread—time enough for damper when the bread ran out—and at once got into their bags just as they were.

'You're not bad at roughing it, Brown, considering your upbringing.' Roper's voice came across the darkness to Georgina.

'My upbringing?' she echoed.

'Home nurturing.' Roper yawned. 'No rise and shine. No long rows of cold showers and boys yelling at the first chilly drops.'

'No, Mr Roper,' she agreed.

'Still, it makes for a kind of bond, I believe, comrades in nakedness. A pity you missed it.'

If you say so, said Georgina under her breath. Aloud she said: 'I guess so, sir.'

'But you can still catch up. Toughen up.'

When? Georgina shivered. Not on this exploration, she hoped!

His next words calmed her.

'But I'm afraid we have our plates full right now. That intrusive was pretty definite, wasn't it?'

'I thought so, sir.'

They talked eagerly for several hours on intrusives and belts and the ever-enthralling 'signs', for they were both of a kind at least in that, then quietly, not even noticing his voice becoming fainter to her, Georgina slipped off to sleep.

She awoke to find him bending over her, and for a moment she was very acutely—and femininely—alarmed.

'George,' he said softly.

'Yes, Mr Roper?'

'Have you seen the Lights?'

115

'The Lights?' She was still drowsy.

'It's not given to every traveller to see the Min-Min Lights, and you're going to see them now. Here, let me give you a pull out.'

But Georgina was up on her feet before he could touch her.

He gave her no quizzical look, for his eyes were on the Lights, and he directed her gaze to where he gazed; in his absorption he did not even seem to notice how she shrank nervously from his indicative touch. Then, with a catch at her heart, Georgina saw what he wanted her to see.

'They're called the Min-Min Lights, George, and there's no explanation for them; in fact mostly they're simply not believed. Those who haven't seen them just can't credit them, either that or they come forward with some practical reason that can't be proved, reasons like satellites, or the sky taking up a reflection from elsewhere and transferring it here.'

'A kind of night mirage?' she asked.

'Yes. Even the ones who *are* given the opportunity are so astounded at the sight that they begin to wonder whether they did witness the miracle.'

'And what about you, Mr Roper?'

'These are my third Min-Min Lights, so I know they're true, but still the magic has never diminished. No man, be he geologist, scientist or explorer, has, or can, explain the Min-Min. But why explain? You don't pull a flower to pieces to see how the petals fit in.'

She had never heard him like this, and as she looked on the mysterious golden glow in the navy plush sky, she felt a magic, too; a wonder, a joy. Yet somewhere there was a regret, unacknowledged at first, then reluctantly but compulsively admitted. I wish, Georgina thought, this could have been under different circumstances. I wish I was Georgina, not George.

'See, they're gone.'

Roper's voice broke into her thoughts, and Georgina

knew wryly it was just as well. Just as well, too, that the Lights were over. She must watch herself, Georgina decided as she got back into her sleeping bag. She must remember that she was George Brown.

It was a good week. There were no tricky moments, nothing to send Georgina hurrying into the scrub to examine a rock for a sign. Clothes were no difficulty, because they simply and unhygienically stayed on.

'When we get back,' said Roper, 'we wallow. Wallow for hours. Bags I first go at the bath.'

'I have my own shower,' she pointed out.

'Which you don't use,' he reminded her drily. 'I told you the tap was turned off.'

'I still bath,' Georgina protested, 'in a basin.'

'Make it a very big basin this time, son; you deserve it, you've worked well and done a good job. So good that I'll let you go first after all.'

'First?'

'In the bath. Unless' ... he grinned ... 'we'll have a communal one. The Japanese recommend it.'

'They soap first and then soak,' she returned.

'Well?'

'I want to do it the other way round.' She was going red, she could feel she was going red, and men didn't.

'Well, we'll see,' he nodded, 'but I won't drop you off at the hut, I'll take you up to the house.'

That was on the final day of the safari, an expedition that had turned out better than Georgina could have hoped.

She found herself humming as they bumped back to Roper's, Larry occasionally asking for a compass reading, for he had taught her how to do it. She had never sung before when she was with him; she knew her speaking voice was convincingly husky, but one never knew when it was a song instead, yet somehow she still had to sing.

'Nice voice, George.' Larry negotiated the jeep round a rock outcrop. 'More tenor than anything else, I'd say, but then that's you, isn't it?'

'I have a deep speaking voice,' she objected.

'Yet overall you're tenor. To put it more to the point you're not what I call a tough guy.'

'You never asked for one.'

'I never asked for a few things that I got,' he returned.

Georgina almost said: 'Like what, Mr Roper?' but that would have been unwise; she might have been *told*. She did not think Roper had any inkling; after this last smooth, congenial week he couldn't have any inkling, yet sometimes he said rather peculiar things . . .

They were in the home territory again now and had no need for the compass. They skirted the hut and made straight for the homestead. As they came within sight of it, Georgina saw that there was someone on the verandah, and that the person was a female and not Mrs Willmott. Not in a slim flame-coloured dress. Larry had seen her, too.

'Who in tarnation——' he began, then he had to concentrate on another detour round some roots.

But Georgina did not join in his curiosity, for by now she knew.

'What is so attractive up there?' her stepsister had said over the telephone. 'I'm coming up to find out what makes a feller like you tick.'

Now she had come as she said and probably found out a little already, and she undoubtedly intended to find out a lot more.

'It's Joanne,' Georgina said.

CHAPTER TEN

THE track was smooth now, so Larry Roper could drive and regard at the same time. He regarded Joanne, then let out an appreciative whistle.

'I say, Brown, she's really something! No wonder you didn't want her up here. Sly devil, aren't you—all that "Stay away" was only against us, against the men, and you were thinking of yourself. You didn't fancy the competition.'

Georgina shook her head. 'You're wrong. I didn't and I don't want Joanne here.'

'But she has still come, hasn't she? For all your innocent expression you really must understand girls, Brown; something I confess I've never done.'

'What do you mean?'

'You've played hard to get, George, and done it very successfully. "Don't come, Joanne" in your case meant "Come at once".'

'She's my stepsister.' Georgina had almost said: 'We're stepsisters.'

'Stick to your story, Brown,' Larry Roper grinned.

'We have different names,' she said, and he laughed.

'Of course. I've never thought of you as Joanne.'

'Different *sur*names,' she said stubbornly, 'Joanne is a Miss Sutherland.'

'Very interesting. Is that why you chose Iain Sutherland for your study?'

'Not *the* reason. It's a common name after all.'

'For an uncommonly beautiful girl.' They were coming nearer to the verandah and the slender figure in flame.

119

'Look, George,' Roper spoke more sympathetically, 'there's no need for you to keep up this stepsister act.'

'She *is* my stepsister!'

Roper ignored Georgina's interruption. 'Also, there's no need to pretend you don't want her, even if you've worked out that it's a good strategy to get her here.'

'Sir, I——'

He ignored her protest. 'Be yourself, son, be honest and go after her. Because I can tell you this, if you don't, and at once, half a dozen of our stalwarts will.'

'Including yourself?'

'Led by me, I'm never included. Surely you have gathered that by now,' Roper said arrogantly. 'A girl like that,' he added, 'deserves the best.'

'Which you are?'

'I'm the boss,' he pointed out.

'Yes, but——' Georgina stopped herself in time from retorting: 'But a boss doesn't have to be the best.'

'You were saying, Brown?' drawled Roper.

'Nothing, sir.' Which was true. All at once Georgina felt nothing. She knew it was all over, all the silly pretence; she had read that doomed men go through agonies, but she just felt numb. She felt quite neutral. She thought of that moment in the bush when she had wished she could be Georgina, not George, but now that she was to be Georgina again there was no excitement, only a desolation. It was because Joanne, beautiful, vital Joanne, was waiting on the verandah. There would be *two* girls, and very soon Larry Roper would know that. He would look at the lovely butterfly that was Joanne, then the brown moth that was Georgina.

Well, and Georgina bit her lip at the thought, at least I hope it gives him a laugh.

They were pulling up. Joanne was coming down to meet them. Thank goodness they never had been kissing sisters ... *step*sisters ... though it couldn't matter now.

Then——

'Greetings, George,' said Joanne. She smiled and held out her hand.

Georgina, absolutely dumbfounded, simply stood.

'Well now, Brown,' reproached Roper, 'you could be more spontaneous in your response. That's what I really call a nice gesture.' He bowed to Joanne. 'After the indifferent way you've spoken about this charming young lady, for her to turn her other cheek as she's doing now just has to be applauded.' Another bow. 'And such a cheek, if I may be so impertinent, Miss Sutherland.'

'If that's meant as a compliment——' said Joanne archly.

'It is.'

'Then I love compliments.' Joanne showed her little white teeth in a sweet smile for Roper alone. He acknowledged it by going across and taking her hand in his.

'You're very welcome, Joanne. May I say Joanne?'

'Oh, please, Mr Roper.'

'Larry. All right, George, are you turned to stone? Action, man, begin to unload.'

Shakingly, disbelievingly, Georgina obeyed.

As she carried their rock spoil into a room off the verandah that Roper had fixed up as a laboratory, Georgina knew that Joanne was watching her; probably with that amused, faintly contemptuous look she always adopted with Georgina, but she dared not look back to find out.

She was not deceived by Joanne's casual greeting, though, and that handshake had been a false one. She's playing with me, Georgina squirmed, she's doing a cat-and-mouse. When it pleases her she will spring the fact of my sex, and she and Roper will have a wonderful laugh together.

But evidently the laugh was not to be heard yet. Once, when Georgina dropped one of the rocks they had brought back for testing and Joanne picked it up, making quite an effort of it in spite of the fact that she was really as strong as a horse and it was not a heavy stone, she came behind her stepsister into the lab with it, saying in a helpful, little-girl voice: 'You dropped this, George.'

Georgina, glancing around and seeing Roper crossing to his men's quarters, said quickly: 'You can drop the pretence, Joanne. He's not here.'

'*She* might be, that gorgon of a housekeeper.'

'Willy is a wonderful woman,' rejoined Georgina.

'I felt she didn't take to me,' Joanne shrugged.

'Well, that doesn't matter, does it?' said Georgina. 'It's the men taking to you that maters.'

'Correction, dear George, man. One man. The big boss. I think that's why your Willy was cool to me. It appears she has successfully done away with three previous contenders.'

'Four.'

'There were only three photos in the lounge.'

'But there was a fourth contender.'

Joanne shrugged again. 'Well, it seems she's handled them and doesn't care about starting on me. Is that why you're acting the man?'

'Of course not.'

'Well, it could look like that, and I'm telling you now, George, if you're doing all this with—well, with something in view, I wouldn't care about it, either.'

'What do you mean?' Georgina inquired hoarsely.

'Simple, I love your Larry Roper. I loved him the minute I saw this wonderful estate. The man must be a near-millionaire. Sly, aren't you, George? You couldn't get in here as a girl—oh, yes, I know the real reason, Bill told me that only a male employee would be acceptable—so you did a change-over trick from woman to man. Rather easy for a feller like you. Really, you're browner and thinner and drier and more up and down than you ever were.'

'A good foil for you.'

'Perhaps, but I'm still not going to risk trying it,' Joanne said calmly.

'Trying it?'

'Trying you as a female against me. Men can be such fools. Most of them go for looks, but not all. The very fact that you've been masquerading successfully possibly could attract Larry Roper ... he seems a different type from the usual run of males ... and I just can't take the chance of any other attraction. Not just now.'

'You mean——'

'I mean, George, that you're remaining *George*. I decided as I came down that very long drive and found this very big house that it would be better that way. Well—until I say so. In other words I won't be giving you away. Not yet.'

Georgina swallowed. 'But it's sure to be found out. You'd forget and tell it to the world.'

'Me?' smiled Joanne pityingly, and that was true, remembered Georgina. Unless she had wanted to, Joanne had never burst out with anything.

'You won't like it here,' Georgina said.

'It will amuse me,' continued Joanne.

'The hut is very meagre.'

'What hut? Oh, where you sleep! Mrs Willmott said you had a bush retreat.'

'Yes, and there's no luxuries. No power, no bath. No——'

'But, foolish boy, I won't be there.'

'Won't be——?'

'I'll be up here, of course, as befits a young lady. Already I have my own room.' Joanne smiled.

'But——'

'I couldn't be with you, anyway, George dear. You may be my step, but you're the wrong sex, remember? Even in remote country places, the middle of nowhere like this, convention matters, and I hardly think a stepsister and a stepbrother sharing the same four walls would be quite the thing.'

'But Joanne——'

'Look, Georgina,' now the teasing had gone out of Joanne and only angry intent remained, 'you got yourself into this, so in you stay. That I have happened along, and that I find it all to my liking, is purely coincidental. *You* started it, so—so—wallow in it. Ah, there's Mr Roper now.

Even without his other advantages he's all right, isn't he? But I forgot, you don't think like that—you're a man, too. Oh, Larry,' Joanne raised her voice, and she had a high, trilling voice, not at all like Georgina's deep tone, 'your lab is simply marvellous! Will you explain it to me one day?'

He grinned. 'No day like today. No time like the present ... that is if you can bear to be near a man who hasn't changed his clothes for almost a week.'

'You smell minty to me, kind of herby. You smell manly,' Joanne said in her slightly breathless manner. 'I love it.'

'Then it's on your shoulders. While I'm showing your stepsister round, Brown, you can have first go at the bathroom. Down at the hut, Joanne, there's no bath, so we've *both* been looking forward to a hot tub. I'll have Willy get some clobber from one of the smaller blokes for you, George. Or perhaps Joanne can help out with a pair of slacks and an overshirt. Not your cup of tea, son, but at least a clean change.'

'No,' said Georgina in agony.

'Don't wonder at your reluctance,' sympathised Roper, 'but no one will see you. Can you help, Joanne?'

'Of course. I've some corduroys, and I've even included some very male-looking shirts. Tabs and military pockets and very, very masculine,' Joanne trilled in that appealing little-girl voice she could adopt. Her small white teeth showed a smile again. 'You know, Larry,' she said confidentially, 'we took the same size growing up. George was never a big boy—he isn't now—and I always envied him his short brown hair. So handy when bathing. I had these wretched long golden curls ...' Joanne's voice was fading away as she moved beside Larry Roper down the verandah to fetch the clothes.

Georgina lost no opportunity. She had been longing for a bath; in fact the thought of hot water all around her had been tantalising her for hours, but now she gave it no second thought. The basin it would be, in the privacy and seclusion of her retreat in the bush.

She waited until they turned into the hall, then she left the lab, left the verandah and the homestead, then began racing down the track.

When she got to the hut she propped a chair against the door, after which she lit the Primus and put on the biggest saucepan of water she could fit over the flame. It would not be the same as a deep bath with endless hot water to top the bath up as it cooled, but at least she was away from the house.

Up there where probably they were now standing on the verandah with the clothes and laughing about her. Then, the subject of George exhausted, looking at each other and not laughing.

Just looking.

After she had bathed, Georgina dressed in clean clothes and waited. She had no doubt that someone would be down to take her up for dinner, or if that didn't happen one of Mrs Willmott's wonderful hampers would arrive. After all, she had lived on brisket for a week.

So Georgina sat on the doorstep and waited.

She watched the sun pass over to the west, turning the rocks into slabs of violet; she saw the evening star prick out. Why, it's night, she realised, and no one has come.

She was so indignant she decided to refuse whatever was offered when it did arrive. She would go to bed and not answer the door when either someone came down to fetch her or to leave some fresh food. She would put out the light and pretend sleep.

She went inside and was in her pyjamas and under the rug within minutes, and there she lay and listened ... listened until it finally came to Georgina that there was nothing to listen to, that at—she looked at her watch— yes, that at half-past nine at night there was going to be nobody and nothing. A great wave of self-pity rushed over her. She felt hot tears pricking down her cheeks.

She lay there until hunger got her up. She went to the fridge and ate something not very appetising, she could not have said what it was, and she ate standing up. Then she went back to bed.

She tried not to think of the house. Dinner by candlelight would be over now; Larry would be entertaining Joanne in the lounge, probably, since she was obviously a feminine girl, playing records. Romantic records. Mrs Willmott would be leaving only the soft wall lights on, getting up and saying: 'If I can be excused.'

What then? Georgina lay there fuming. What then up there, while she, who had worked so hard, lay alone and unnourished down here?

Suddenly unable to stay quiet any more, Georgina got up and dressed sketchily. She took the torch and went out of the hut and up the track. She had no idea of what she intended doing or even whether she had any intention at all. She simply stumbled on. At the first sight of the lights of the homestead, she thought vaguely, I'll stop. Then I'll come back. If there are no house lights on I'll—I'll——

A hand gripped her, and Georgina only just stopped a scream. Girls scream, men don't, she was thinking automatically as she faced the mighty Roper.

'What in heaven do you think you're at, Brown?' He sounded quite frighteningly angry. 'Are you sleepwalking?'

'No,' she stumbled, 'I mean, I don't think so. I mean, I left something up here.'

'Wouldn't it wait till the morning?'

'I didn't think so, but I do now. I—I'll come back later, sir.'

'Not so fast.' He put a hand on Georgina's arm, quite a light touch, but there was an intention there.

'Y-yes, sir?'

'I'll walk down with you,' Roper said. 'In fact,' as they started off, 'I was coming hours ago. When you didn't turn up for dinner I put your absence down to being dog-tired. You worked like a hero this week.'

'Thank you, sir,' she answered stiffly.

'I decided not to disturb you, not even with a food

hamper, not for an hour or so. I decided to let you relax, then I would see how you were. At least'—a shrug—'that's what I *intended*, Brown.'

'Sir?' She looked up at him.

'Does your stepsister always—does she——'

'Yes, sir?'

'Is she always such a talker? Oh, she's charming, George, don't misunderstand me, but I've been trying to get down to see if you were all right all night.'

'You have, sir?' Her heart glowed. They were approaching the hut now.

'You'll find a hamper on the table,' Roper told Georgina. 'I must have got here just after you left. I came through the scrub.'

'Thank you, sir.' Georgina opened the door.

She had expected Roper to leave her, and she didn't mind any more if he did. It wasn't just the fact of the food, it was the fact that he hadn't forgotten her after all. All the time they had been playing records ... or it might have been all the time that Joanne had been talking ... he had been remembering her down here. It was a nice feeling, she found.

But Roper had come in and he was lighting the lamp, and when he finished that he lit the primus.

'Put out the nosh, Brown,' he tossed at her.

'I thought you'd eaten, sir.'

'Yes, by candlelight. But the fact is, George, I've become used to a different light. Lamplight.'

Georgina said: 'It was lantern light out there.'

'I've become used to—well, basics. I've become used to——' He stopped.

'Used to brisket on bread?' Georgina felt she had to break something up, though what was to be broken up she wasn't sure, but it mustn't go any further.

'No, I'll do without that brisket,' he grinned. Then all at once he wasn't grinning, he was looking at her.

127

'I guess you could say, George,' he said, 'I've got used to you.'

The hamper held chicken, fresh butter, salad, bread and cheese. They ate together, but they said very little. There seemed nothing to be needed to be said. There was nothing at all to make Georgina happy, yet she knew she could have reached up and plucked every star out of the sky. She knew she had never felt so wonderful in all her life.

They finished the last crumb and drank the last drop of tea, then Roper went up to the homestead and Georgina went back to bed. She slept, and she slept happily ... happily ...

The next day she knew it had all been a fantasy, for Joanne strolled down, and the happiness lay as limp as a balloon with a hole.

'How did the midnight feast go?' Joanne began slyly. 'I mean your side of it, George. Larry's already told me his.' She started to laugh. 'Hilarious,' she said between spasms.

'He told you?'

'Of course. Did you think I didn't know he was coming? It was my idea. We were sitting in the lounge and I said: "Larry, why don't you take something down to my poor stepbrother, after all we've had a wonderful night, yet poor George——"'

'Well, as you know now, he went. He told me all about it.' Joanne laughed again. 'You two sitting in this ugly little room having your midnight feast just like two naughty school boarders tucking into a forbidden hamper! Larry was convulsed. Oh, I'm sorry, George!'

'Sorry?'

'Larry did mention that you seemed to be very serious over it all. You must forgive me, but I can't help it. We laughed and laughed.' Joanne dabbed at her eyes now.

'Yes,' said Georgina, 'I'm sure.'

After a few minutes Joanne, still giggling at the memory, appealed: 'Forgotten, George?'

'Of course. Joanne—Joanne, I'll be leaving soon.'

'You'll what?' Joanne looked startled.

'You heard me.' Georgina spoke sharply. 'I'll be leaving here.'

'Why?'

'I've had enough.'

'You really mean you don't want to stay on now I'm here—you mean you can see no future in it. Was there any before?'

'I am leaving, Joanne,' Georgina repeated.

'Oh, no, you're not. If you leave, there's nothing, nothing ostensible, I mean, to keep me here. And I intend to stay.'

'Won't Mr Roper keep you here?' asked Georgina dully.

'Eventually, most certainly, but I can't move too quickly, he's not that kind of man.'

'Then don't think that I could do the trick for you. Why, he doesn't even believe we're related, not really.'

'I've told him we are,' corrected Joanne. 'He believes me.'

'Nice for you.'

'Very nice.' Joanne studied her hands. 'No, George, you're staying on, otherwise I tell him the trick you've played.'

'That won't affect me,' Georgina said.

'I wouldn't be certain. Anyway, I wouldn't like to be in your shoes when he found out that you'd taken him for a fool. He is' . . . a little smile . . . 'a very authoritative kind of man.'

'My word for him is arrogant.'

'I like some arrogance.' Joanne smiled again.

'Well, it still doesn't keep me here. You don't.'

'But lack of money would, and you don't have any money, do you? Also, your next pay is already earmarked for me.'

Georgina stiffened. 'Joanne——'

'That van—— You might have thought you were clever giving it to that storekeeper for food, but you won't think you're so clever when you get a summons. And I'd do it, you know me.'

'Oh, yes, I know you.'

'And why not?' Joanne continued hotly. 'I got nothing from Father, absolutely nothing. You in your sly way bagged it all.'

'I didn't! You know I didn't.' Georgina was almost crying.

'I don't know, and I'll see to it that other people also "don't know"; that's unless you conform, and by conforming I mean staying on until I say you can go.' A pause. 'Larry and I are going out today. He intends to show me around. No doubt he'll feel obliged to invite his so-called geo, after all you are the only non-cattle employee on the station, but no doubt,' with significance, 'you will say no.'

'I will say no,' Georgina concurred. She said it quite docilely, for something had occurred to her. With Joanne and Roper away for the day there was nothing to stop her from leaving, really leaving. She was fully aware that everything that Joanne had said she could do to her she could do, and aware that Larry Roper would be terribly angry; but she, thought Georgina, would not be here. Let them sort it out between themselves when they get back from their outing.

As Joanne had anticipated, Roper same down later and invited Georgina to accompany them.

'Not an exploration, not anything really,' he smiled.

'No, thank you, I have some notes to write up.'

'I suppose so. Well, please yourself, Brown.' He gave a little wave and went off.

Once more Georgina packed her bags and put them by the door, filled the haversack to stow at the back of the bike seat. It was becoming a routine, she thought, but this time it would happen. She tidied the hut, finished the data Roper would need on the rocks they had brought in from the safari and left them on the table for him. After lunch, when Mrs Willmott was resting and the stockmen flat on their backs, when even the dogs were asleep, she would take off on the bike. She did not think how she would get the bike back to Roper's; that would come later.

It all went as she planned. In the inertia of midday Georgina drove off, and did not go quietly by the homestead. If Willy did see her she would only think that George was taking a spin.

Out on the road at last, the road she had come up with Craig, Georgina turned north, wondering how far the Brydens were, how they would react to her, how long it would be before Craig called at his property and took her with him.

The road was as straight as an arrow, not a bend anywhere, but there were detours as always, round rock outcrops, ditches, sticky patches.

Coming out of one of these, Georgina saw a car bearing down on her from the opposite direction, and she laughed with delight. She would have recognised that car anywhere. Why not? Hadn't she slept in it?

Craig saw her an instant after she saw him, and he applied his brakes.

'Of all the sights for sore eyes!' he greeted, and he leapt out and kissed her warmly.

'Oh, Craig!' Georgina greeted him.

'Where are you bound?' he asked.

'The Brydens'. For you to pick me up. You said you would, remember?'

'Of course, but I don't know now, Georgina. I'm not a popular man there, so naturally you wouldn't be a popular girl. Or,' a grin, 'whatever you are now.'

'But why are you unpopular, Craig? What have you done?' she asked.

'Nothing. I always do nothing, but, like the rest of this wretched district, it's nothing but the mighty Roper on everybody's lips, and seeing that Roper despises me, I guess the disease has spread.'

'Poor Craig! But not to worry, I'll just come with you as I am and leave out the Brydens.'

'Then welcome, kid. *Not* a Roper devotee, I take it. Has it been that bad?' he inquired.

131

'Worse.' She made a face.

'And yet there's been talk about you. I even got quite jealous.'

'Jealous?'

'There was a beautiful girl at Roper's, the talk went.'

'Then you should have known it wasn't me,' Georgina grimaced.

'Of course it was you,' he argued, 'who else?'

'My stepsister,' said Georgina, 'has arrived. *She's* a beauty.'

Craig looked thoughtful. 'Interesting, but alas not for me, Roper would see to that. Talk of the devil, here comes the Roper car now.'

Georgina blinked into the distance and saw a car a long distance away. It might be Roper's, she said doubtfully, but still it mightn't be.

'It's his. It's the only model of that sort in these parts. Hi, what are you doing?' For Georgina was wheeling the bike behind the car, getting into the car and lying down.

Before Craig could say any more, Roper's car was abreast of them, and then it had gone on.

'Safe?' called Georgina.

Craig did not answer.

'Safe?' Georgina peered out for herself and saw that it was. She got out of the car and came to the man who was following the Roper blob of dust with a rather stunned expression.

'How can I get the bike back when I come with you?' Georgina asked.

There was no answer.

'Wake up, Craig, I'm asking you a question! How can we get the bike back to Roper's now I'm coming with you?'

'Simple, sweetheart.' Craig looked down on Georgina. 'You're not coming with me. You're getting back on the bike and going home at once, and making believe you never left. Now I know why they spoke of a beautiful girl—why, she's fantastic! And you're staying on to introduce her to me.'

'I'm not!' Georgina exclaimed hotly.

'But Georgina——'

'No!'

'Then' ... a sigh ... 'it was just a lovely idea of mine. Goodbye, Georgina.' He looked significantly at her, and she gasped.

'Craig, you promised to help me, take me away.'

'And I will, in return for my meeting that beauty. I'll take you back to Sydney whenever you like, but you have to let us meet first.'

'I'm beginning to understand,' Georgina said slowly, 'why Larry Roper despises you and the Brydens dislike you. I think I hate you myself.'

He grinned. 'Yet you need me, pet, as I need you. I must meet—what's her name?'

'Joanne. And why must you, Craig?' As he didn't answer Georgina went on: 'Another string to your bow? Like Elva?'

'Darling, no girl is ever like the one before, and please don't believe all you hear. And now home with you, Georgina, for I've another sales call to make down the track. If you don't go back, frankly I don't know what you'll do. There won't be another car through today. Think it over.' He blew her a kiss, got into the car and left.

For a while Georgina just stood there, then she got back on the bike.

She reached the hut and just had time to put back her stacked belongings before Joanne strolled down.

'A boring day,' Joanne pronounced feelingly. 'I must say I find rocks as interesting as cattle, and they're the most uninteresting things in the world. But I did see one interesting thing—a very good-looking man on the road. Evidently Larry recognised and disliked him, for he accelerated as we went past. He was a real winner, George; he didn't seem the stodgy station type, he looked smarter, more cityfied. Do they have travellers up here?'

'Yes.'

'Would you know this one?' Joanne persisted.

'Yes. Yes, Joanne, I do.'

'Then see to it that we meet. Nothing to it, of course, but I must have something, some diversion, or I'll die of boredom before——'

'Before?' Georgina asked sharply.

But Joanne only smiled.

'See to it,' she said again as she went out.

It seemed, Georgina thought, that the interest was mutual on both sides, on Joanne's and on Craig's.

And why not? Why not do as they asked? It appeared the only way she would ever *really* leave this place.

CHAPTER ELEVEN

JOANNE settled herself gracefully into the homestead life, a source of joy for the cattlemen, who found numerous excuses to present themselves at the verandah steps, ostensibly to ask the boss something but really to gaze on the beautiful creature that had come among them. Since she enjoyed their admiration, and since it cost her nothing, Joanne rewarded them with a dazzling smile.

Larry Roper, too, for all his chance admission on that first night that Joanne talked too much, was apparently as smitten as the rest. Georgina never saw him unless he had her stepsister with him, and after a few days he had her hanging on his arm, which rather contradicted Joanne's statement that he was not the type to move quickly, Georgina thought.

In fact the only one apart from herself who was not seemingly bewitched with Joanne was Willy. Mrs Willmott didn't take to her, in fact she disliked her, and she told Georgina so.

'You two are as different as chalk and cheese,' she muttered resentfully.

'Well, Willy, we're not blood relations.'

'Yes, but you grew up together, I've heard you say, and often something rubs off. Well, nothing of you rubbed off on her, George, and I'm pleased to say vice versa. How long is Madam staying?'

'I don't know. Until Mr Roper says she goes, I suppose.'

Mrs Willmott frowned. 'She's put him on a spot. He's a gentleman and he wouldn't like to tell her to go, especially when she's a connection of yours.'

135

All this considerably surprised Georgina. First the possibility of the mighty Roper letting himself get put on a spot: second, his gentlemanliness, that would prevent him taking a stand against a woman. Third, and most important of all, Willy's opinion that he would even consider his humble geologist.

'After his past experience' . . . that should be experiences, plural, Georgina thought, recalling the three other girls in the photos besides Elva . . . 'it's not fair to put him through another. I know my Mr Larry, and she—Miss Sutherland —definitely is not the one for him,' said Mrs Willmott firmly.

'Is there a one?' Georgina asked.

'Yes, George, I rather think there is, but I don't know her, and I'm just sensing this. He could have met her on one of his trips, but there's still someone, I'm sure. A woman always knows.'

'I don't.' Georgina just stopped that in time. 'Woman's intuition,' she said aloud instead.

'Well, maybe,' shrugged Willy, 'and maybe it's only wishful thinking on my part for Mr Roper. I admit I don't want to see him take up with your stepsister, George. I don't like her and I don't trust her. Also, the longer she stays here the harder it will be to get her out; people get entrenched. Can't *you* do anything about it?'

'No, Mrs Willmott, I can't,' Georgina said simply.

'Then I suppose we'll just have to wait and hope that her boredom—for she is bored, you know—finally comes to a head, and that she'll get sick of waiting and takes off with someone else instead.'

'Someone up here?'

'It's been done before,' said Mrs Willmott cryptically, and left it at that.

That her dislike of Joanne was not a passing mood was established a few days later by her pointblank refusal to put on a barn-dance for the visitor. Larry Roper told Georgina so when he came down one day to the hut to pick up Georgina's reports.

'I don't like what's got into Willy, she's usually the most generous soul and never spares herself when it comes to providing for a party, but when I suggested a night for your stepsister, she turned it down.'

'It's a lot of work,' excused Georgina.

'Willy thrives on work. No, she just wouldn't be in on it. I would insist, for after all it's an accepted thing out here to share your guest around—especially such a guest as Joanne—except that it's all been taken out of my hands.'

'You mean the men are doing it on their own accord?' inquired Georgina, and he shook his head.

'My men, as you must have noted by now, Brown, are almost without exception the maturer type. Even the younger ones are old compared with you and your stepsister. Oh, no, they're not putting on anything. They're quite content to look upon Joanne now and then and be glad that they can do so without ruin to their pockets, for undoubtedly a girl like that would ruin a man's pockets. I pay high salaries up here, but the money is hard toil and the men appreciate that, and mostly their wages go to some private goal. I've no doubt that every member of my employ is out for what he can get and as much as he can get with a definite end in view, and good luck to them, I say.'

'Yes,' nodded Georgina. 'Then where is the party to be held?'

'East of Roper's, a big holding, though not so big as ours. Fortescues'. There'll be the usual crowd there, plus the lovely ladies and our loveliest lady. She will be the draw,' Roper smiled.

'Drawing you?' asked Georgina.

'Not drawing me. I've never been much of a socialiser, and I won't be there. You see,' grinning, 'when it comes to dancing I have two left feet. Also, I doubt if the men will go.'

'But they enjoyed our barn-dance.'

'It was here, and that's a big thing when you're working

137

flat out as they are. That drive home afterwards over a hundred kilometres can be a killer. But I expect you and Joanne to represent Roper's, Brown.'

'Joanne won't care for that at all,' said Georgina, 'being accompanied by her step . . . stepbrother.'

'I think she'll like it. Well, she'll have to, either that or miss out. You can grab some other girl as soon as you get there, and leave her to her own conquests.'

Georgina shifted. 'I'm afraid like you, sir, I'm no socialiser.'

'Then at least we have something in common as well as rock,' he laughed. 'Not to worry, Brown, you can always conduct your choice to some nook under the stars.'

About to say something concerning that, too, Georgina desisted, and the conversation left the forthcoming party and got back to business again. Roper said that he had planned another safari, but a brief one this time, and its purpose was to make a second search on their finds before he went down to register a claim.

'It's an extremely expensive business,' he said, 'so I want to be absolutely certain. I feel confident, but I must be cautious. How are your feelings, George?'

'I feel certain,' she agreed.

'But you agree I should check?'

'By all means double-check,' Georgina advised wholeheartedly, especially wholeheartedly because she knew she could give the advice with an easy mind. She had no qualms about going out there with him any more, not on an all-absorbing geological search.

'You'll doubtless hear from the Fortescues,' Roper tossed at her, then he rose and left the hut.

Joanne was excited about the party; at least it would be a break in the boredom, she said.

'If you don't like it here now,' Georgina said once, 'how can you expect to change your mind if, and when, later on you—well——'

'Become Mrs Roper?'

'Yes.'

'Then no ifs, George, and *when* is getting closer every day. As for liking it, it will be different then. We'll only come out here on occasion, and live in the city as lots of men like Larry do.'

'But such men aren't Larry.'

A hard glitter came into Joanne's eyes. 'You seem to know a lot about him, George. So long as it's strictly man to man?'

'Oh, it's man to man,' Georgina assured her, and was dismayed at the bitter note she detected in her voice. She looked quickly at Joanne to see her reaction, but, typical of Joanne, in her vain self-absorption she had not heard.

'I'll wear my pink,' she was planning, 'I'll be femininity itself. These westerners are woman-starved.'

'Not really, there'll be cars and trucks driving in from miles away, and a lot of them will carry some very pretty girls.'

Joanne smiled pityingly at Georgina for making such a stupid statement, then she asked: 'What about you?'

'Well, what about me?'

'You're coming, aren't you?'

'It appears it's expected of me. You see, Mr Roper won't be there.'

Joanne was unperturbed. 'No, I didn't think it would be his cup of tea, and I can't say I'm very disappointed. He'd be rather a damper at a party, or at least to me. He's certainly not the party type. Now I'll be able to let myself go, play the field.' She looked at Georgina again. 'You never answered. What about you?'

'I'm going.'

'I know. But—as George?'

'Oh, don't be silly, Joanne, how can I go as anything else?'

'But a bit risky, isn't it? I mean, mingling as we're presumably expected to mingle.'

139

'I won't be mingling,' Georgina said, 'I'll be waiting in the car.'

'Wise girl—I mean wise boy. I only hope the night doesn't seem interminable to you.' Joanne paused. 'Do you think it's likely that—that man will be there?'

'Which man?'

'Oh, don't be infuriating, George, you know I mean that man we passed on the road.'

'He could be,' admitted Georgina.

'Can't you do better than that? Can't you contact him and tell him he should go?'

'No, I can't. To begin with he's not in high favour at Roper's.'

'That needn't matter, because they needn't know.'

'Joanne, I couldn't tell him because I don't know where he is! He leases his station to the Brydens while he travels for some farm machinery firm in Melbourne. The Brydens are the next holding north, but that's all I know.'

Joanne shrugged. 'Simple, then, he's sure to call in at these Brydens if only to collect his dues.'

'They don't particularly like him.'

Joanne shrugged again. 'They would still be obliged to pass on your message.'

'No,' refused Georgina.

Joanne, about to argue, evidently changed her mind, and though Georgina did not trust the little smile she wore, she let it pass.

There were some moments of unease for Georgina when Larry Roper reported that all the men save one had turned down the Fortescue invitation.

'Pat Dawson is going,' he said, 'he's sweet on a girl from The Downs. He met her at our own party. I was glad when I found out about Pat being there, otherwise I think I would have had second thoughts.'

'About our going?' she asked.

'No—I wanted, and still want, Joanne to have that experience.' No mention of her, Georgina noticed. 'No, my second thoughts were concerning myself. I didn't fancy you driving there alone, Brown, I mean driving your stepsister. By the way, I'm presuming that you do drive a car? You're certainly a whizz on bikes.'

'I drive,' Georgina said shortly.

'But now Pat can take you.'

'Yes,' said Georgina unhappily. She could see Pat leaping out of the car when they got to the Fortescues', and sweeping George with him to meet the boys. She could see big pints of beer, feel slaps on the back, see girls being brought across. Larry Roper cut in: 'Not that Pat will even be aware of you once you're there. He's got it badly, I'm afraid.'

Georgina hid her relief.

Joanne was in high spirits. Once Georgina warned her that perhaps her spirits were too high; it was more likely than not, since Craig wasn't a popular figure up here, that he would not be there. He might not even know about it. Possibly, and probably, by this time he was back in the city.

'No,' said Joanne, and a dimple formed in one cheek, something that had always happened when she had got her own way, 'he's not. He'll be there.'

'You can't know,' objected Georgina.

'I'd take a bet on it. You see he does know, George. I rang his place, the Brydens'.'

'*You* did?'

'I said: "Kindly inform Mr Everson from Mr Brown there there will be something for him at Fortescues' next Saturday".'

'Joanne, you didn't!'

Joanne just displayed her triumphant dimple again. 'Pink for an ingénue?' she pondered. 'Or blue, since men like it?'

In the end she wore red. A glowing ruby red guaranteed to put all the other pastel-clad females into the pale doldrums. She looked beautiful and vital and desirable, and Georgina wondered what Larry Roper was thinking. He wasn't there, for he had had a call from one of his trucking gangs that the Roper thirty-six wheeler, as these gargantuan transports were called, had broken down a hundred kilometres to the south, so Roper had left to help effect repairs.

Joanne did not seem unduly upset by this, nor by the fact that her stunning appearance would have to be wasted on someone else. Wasted was Georgina's word. She felt she understood Joanne, and the Joanne she knew never staged anything unless there were strings attached. Yet Joanne, as she whirled her red skirts round, seemed pleased enough.

Georgina went in clean pants and loose clean overshirt. She had expected criticism from Mrs Willmott about this—'Wear something bright at least, George'—but Mrs Willmott did not even come out to the verandah to wish them a happy night. Pat, too, was too self-absorbed to notice either of them.

'I met Jenny,' he related to anyone who would listen, 'at our do, and I thought to myself at once: "She's the girl." I didn't mean to fall yet, I wanted to pile up a bit of dough, but——'

'Shut the window,' broke in Joanne, 'I'm getting blown about.'

It took an hour to get to the Fortescue sign, and once they passed the gate it was snail's pace to the homestead because of the number of cars. Was one of them Craig's? Georgina wondered.

A paddock close to the party barn had been reserved for parking, and as soon as Pat stopped the car he was out and making for the source of the music, by the old-time beat of it the same musicians that Roper's had had. No need to have worried on Pat's account, Georgina smiled to herself, there would be no male back-slapping, no big pints, no introducing of the new Roper geo. Jenny was Pat's only goal.

Joanne followed just as eagerly but not so fast. It was typical of Joanne that she needed no one to present her, for which Georgina should have been relieved and indeed was, but did Joanne have to be quite so sure of herself? She

142

watched her stepsister as she hesitated with a winning show of shyness at the barn door, then Joanne disappeared.

Georgina sat back in the car and gave the party an hour, then she went quietly over to stand in the shadows and watch the scene.

Joanne was not there.

The scene was like all party scenes, probably the same as the scene she had missed at Roper's, and Georgina enjoyed it for a while, but when some of the men emerged for a smoke she decided she would be safer back in the car.

As she started across to the parking paddock, the light from a late arrival lit up the exterior, and she knew why she hadn't seen Joanne, for Joanne had certainly wasted no time. She must have met Craig Everson at once, for the two of them were talking together on the lawn. Very close together.

In another moment the car light was off, but, having seen, Georgina went back to their own car for her long wait.

She stretched out when she got in the back seat, then closed her eyes. With luck she would shorten her waiting hours with sleep. But——

'Are your two left feet troubling you, Brown?' asked a voice, and blinking her eyes open again, Georgina saw that Roper was opening the door of the car. 'I was returning from the repair job,' he said, 'and thought that as I was as near as the Fortescues' gate I would come further and see how you enjoyed yourselves.'

'How did you find me? I mean find your car?' There must be over fifty vehicles parked, Georgina thought.

'I saw you in my headlights, so I promptly followed you.' If he had seen her, he must have seen Joanne, too, Georgina thought. 'I've left my car outside the parking paddock, but I'm not stopping. I've had a gruelling day. A successful one, though, we got the trailer back on its many wheels again with no cattle mishaps. Listen.' He held up his hand. 'Isn't that our song?' he grinned.

Across from the barn echoed Irving Berlin's *Always*.

I'm all for always. Are you? In her mind Georgina heard him say that again.

All at once, and Georgina longed desperately for seclusion, a tear was trickling down her cheek. Thank heaven at least for the dark, she thought, but in case he did see that tear in the glint of a star or when the moon escaped a cloud, Georgina mumbled: 'I think I've gone and got a cold.'

She felt as she had felt on the safari, longing . . . yearning . . . to be Georgina, not George.

'In that case you can come home with me and do all the usual things, rum, lemon and aspirin. Can't have our best geo down with the wog.'

'I'm the only geo,' she pointed out.

'So you have to be the best, don't you?' He was opening the car door. 'I'll find Pat and tell him to bring our lady back in due course.'

'No. Please don't bother. I'll be all right.'

'In your own bed you will. What's wrong with you, Brown? You needn't worry about your stepsister, she would be quite self-reliant, I'm sure. Anyway, Pat knows he has to get himself and her back.'

'Yes, but——'

There was a moment's silence, then Roper said clearly: 'If you think I may be leaving Joanne in the company of someone I don't approve of, then perish your concern. Joanne is a very beautiful girl, and if someone else realises that then I can scarcely object. Now wait here.'

He was not gone long. He came back, said: 'All's well,' and held open the door for Georgina to transfer to his other car, still parked on the drive.

'So you found Pat?' asked Georgina.

'In the arms of his Jenny, yes.'

'Did you find——'

'Joanne? No. But the message will be passed on. Now stop talking, give your throat a rest. When we get back it's a double rum for you.'

'No, sir,' she protested.

144

'Afraid, Brown?'

'Afraid?'

'That you'll talk?' he said.

'But you just told me not to talk.'

'There is talk,' Larry Roper replied, 'and talk.' He concentrated on weaving between other party-going cars that had only got as far as the drive. But once out of the Fortescue gate he pressed down on the accelerator, and they were back at Roper's in less than the hour it had taken them to go to the party.

Much to Georgina's relief Roper drove straight to the hut; she had not looked forward to sitting in the homestead lounge while Roper administered the promised double rum. The telltale light might have found that tear mark on her face, for tears generally showed, and men don't cry.

Then she saw that Roper was coming into the hut behind her. He lit the lamp—no searching light there—then he said: 'Instead of that rum, George, how about a cuppa?'

'Oh yes, yes!' Georgina nearly fell over herself with relief and eagerness.

They drank very leisurely with the door open, and the warm herby, minty air stealing in. They spoke very little.

'After we check our finds, George,' Roper said, 'I'll be going south for several weeks, making dead sure my claims are waterproof. Anything you'd like me to bring back for you? I'll be going by car, so I'll have room.'

Across the table Georgina looked at Larry Roper and wondered what he would say if suddenly she blurted:

'Yes, something pink, please, that's for an ingénue. Or should it be blue because men like it?'

What was he waiting for her to answer? A bottle of after-shave? A plug of tobacco?

'No, nothing, Mr Roper, nothing at all. I—I have everything.'

'Everything, George?' he questioned.

Somewhere far away a dog howled, a yellow dog that must have evaded the dingo fence and was now in forbidden land.

And that's where I'm straying, thought Georgina, I'm getting too close to forbidden land. But oh, how I wish——

'You wish what, George?' Good heavens, had she said that "I wish" aloud?

'I wish,' blurted Georgina, 'I was in bed. I think I feel a little worse. If you don't mind going, Mr Roper——'

'I'm gone,' he nodded sympathetically. 'Lie in tomorrow. I'll even come down myself to see that you've done so.'

Which means, groaned Georgina, getting into the bed she had said she needed but now did not want any more, that I'll have to be up well before that, because——

But it was Joanne who came down, and by that time Georgina was up, 'basin'ed' and breakfasted.

Joanne came in and sat down at the table.

'Pour me some coffee,' she groaned, 'I'm still a little out of this world after last night.'

'Did Pat bring you home?'

'Yes.' Joanne made a face.

'I saw you—with Craig. You had no trouble finding him?'

'My dear George, we simply gravitated to each other,' Joanne said airily.

'So it appeared.'

'How do you mean?'

'I saw you in a car light.'

'Oh!'

'Mr Roper's car light,' Georgina said significantly.

Joanne looked up quickly. She did not seem pleased now.

'Mr Roper is going to the city,' Georgina said at once. She had no wish to start any post-mortems, and her tactics succeeded.

'Is he now?' Joanne said, and she sounded interested.

'Yes, after we get back from our safari this week. It won't be a long one, really only to—well——'

'Well, what?'

'To look around.'

'You've just looked.' Joanne sounded accusing.

'Yes, but findings have to be authenticated.'

'Findings of what?'

Sorry she had started this, Georgina mumbled, 'Nickel.' Then she said: 'As it's not a long trip perhaps you'd like to come too?'

'As chaperone?' inquired Joanne.

'Hardly. Shouldn't that be my role?'

'I don't know. Don't ask me just now.'

'But would you care to come?' Georgina persisted.

'No.'

'It's wonderful country.'

'I see enough of it here.'

'Joanne!'

'Well, that's how I feel, George. I feel sixty in this place. It's so quiet, so dull. I mean, it was until——' she broke off.

'Joanne, don't do anything you'll be sorry about.'

'Oh, I won't,' Joanne smiled.

'And you won't come?'

'You know, George, I think I'll be finding a lot to occupy me back here. And now tell me about this trip. It's a check-up, isn't it?'

'I never said so.'

'But you're going over the same territory, so it must be.'

'Well—yes.'

'Then it must be something big!'

'Let's say promising,' Georgina hedged.

'And Roper—and Larry is making absolutely sure. Yes, that would be like him.' Joanne's bottom lip had thrust out; she did not look so pretty now.

'I'm going out in my car for a Cook's,' she announced.

'Cook's?' echoed Georgina.

'Cook's tour, silly. At least that's what I told Larry. He said to take you along in case I felt bushed, but you aren't coming, are you?'

'Aren't I?'

'No, because I won't be on a Cook's, I'm meeting Craig. Now, George dear, I'm so sorry you refused, but since you insist ... perhaps next time. See you again.' Before Georgina could utter a word, Joanne was gone. Georgina watched her from the door of the hut, then came slowly back into the room.

CHAPTER TWELVE

SEVERAL times that week Georgina saw Joanne's mini-car buzzing down the long pepper-bordered drive to the Roper gates and the north–south road up which she had travelled with Craig, and where Joanne now ostensibly conducted her Cook's tours. Georgina's heart could have gone out to Larry Roper in sympathy for what was being done to him, had she not been unsure whether he did not know already. She could not imagine anything escaping that astute man. And yet, she reasoned, I've scored one over him myself. If she had, then feasibly Joanne had, too. Poor Larry Roper, she thought.

There was no day set yet for the departure of the second checking expedition; something had cropped up on the pastoral side of Roper's that needed the boss's immediate attention. One evening Joanne came down to the hut wearing a thunderous expression, and Georgina found out the reason for her bad temper. Whereas Larry Roper had accepted Joanne's sweet excuses for not looking at rocks, it now appeared he had insisted she accompany the posse that was leaving the next day to overland a mob of the cattle.

'But why?' asked Georgina, puzzled.

'He said I'd better get an idea of what life was really like up here.'

Georgina flinched at that, but hid it. She said brightly: 'I should have thought you would have been pleased at such a statement. It seems a very good sign.'

'The only signs I like are those other signs, George, signs with dollars written all over them, the signs of the miracle nickel. Everyone knows that beef is down in value now.'

'By signs I really meant,' Georgina took a breath and finished, 'matrimonial signs.'

Joanne looked sulkily away and did not comment.

'Will you come, too, George?' she appealed.

'I haven't been instructed. I'm an employee, remember.'

'Well, come anyway,' said Joanne, still sulky. 'I don't want any of those clods getting the wrong idea about me.'

'Which clods? What wrong idea?'

'The stockmen. A female in their midst could start a lot of things, especially one like me.' Joanne said it quite matter-of-factly; she always had been fully aware of her looks.

'But it wouldn't happen with Mr Roper there, too. I mean, they would know.'

'Know what?'

'That you—that he——' Georgina faltered.

'Oh, for heaven's sake, George, stop harping on that. Just see to it that you come, too.'

'What good would I be? Another man?'

'Just come. I might need you,' retorted Joanne.

'But if Mr Roper doesn't require me——'

But Mr Roper, an hour later, told Georgina he would require her.

'I was hoping to get away on our geo business, Brown, but this other has cropped up. I'm taking Joanne, too, to-morrow, for several reasons. Firstly, I want her to know what makes things tick up here.'

'Yes,' said Georgina rather faintly, for she had a hollow feeling inside of her, 'I think that's very wise.'

'Secondly——' He broke off abruptly and was silent for a moment. Then he asked sharply: 'Where does your step-sister go when she buzzes off in her car every day?'

Georgina hesitated. 'She—looks around.'

'Evidently she doesn't register much of what she sees from what she relates when she gets back. That fellow she met at the dance——'

'What fellow?'

'Oh, don't give me that, Brown, you know the one I mean.'

'Well, yes, I do know,' she admitted.

'Is he still around?'

'How should I know?'

He did not answer, but Georgina, who had lowered her eyes, could feel his eyes boring into her. She could not look up; she did not dare to. So he *is* aware of Craig, she thought miserably, and he's unhappy because—well, because he loves Joanne. He must do to be concerned like this, otherwise he wouldn't bother.

'She'll be better with us,' Roper said shortly.

'And you'll take her, too, on the geo check?' Georgina asked quite calmly, and she wondered how she did so. Not there, she was thinking intently, never there, not in that wonderland where the two of us, no one else, once looked up and saw the Min-Min Lights.

'No!' he came in quite forcibly, and this time she did look at him. But he glanced away at once, saying: 'A check is a check. No third person is needed there.'

'Even one who's going to be——'

His eyes narrowed. 'Yes, Brown?'

... Even one who is going to be connected with it? with its riches? marry into it? were Georgina's thoughts, but she did not speak them.

'I'm sure you're right, sir,' she said instead. She changed the subject adroitly. 'What is it that's cropped up on the cattle side? I mean, if it's not secret.'

'You can't be secret about four legs and two horns,' he grinned. 'It's simple, really. We are, as you know, right now the victims of a situation that's affecting all the beef farmers.'

'The beef slump?'

'Yes. The beasts that are ready to road train south are naturally accounted for, but the way nature is there are many more *not* ready.'

'What do you mean?' she queried.

151

'The adolescents, the mothers-to-be, the new mothers with their progeny. For they do multiply, Brown, a habit with property cattle.' A wry laugh. 'We've too many young to keep here until they can grow up and be taken off our hands. A paddock, after all, is exhaustible.'

'Are all cattle stations facing this situation?'

'Since the American and Japanese markets have faded out, yes. But not all are as affected as Roper's, because things have got to the stage where in most places new calves are being knocked on the head as soon as they are born. It has become a sad but necessary precaution when sales are down and overstocking a monstrous certainty. I haven't done that.' His face firmed. 'I never will. But I still can't keep them all here until they're ready for a shrunken, indifferent and even non-existent market. There wouldn't be any fodder left on the place. So we're droving them out, Brown. The gang that goes tomorrow will be relieved in ten days. In another ten days they, too, will step down. I've prepared a roster. You see, under the existing law,' he explained 'unless you can find a sympathetic farmer with more grass than he wants, which is very unlikely, the herd has to be moved each day, but not more than six miles. At night, if you haven't found a good samaritan willing to let you use his fields, or a public yard, you have to fence them in. Well' ... a shrug ... 'it isn't all that hard. We carry wire and sledgehammers and can run up an enclosure by the time a billy boils.'

'Any more rules?' asked Georgina eagerly. She was fascinated by the conversation.

'No droving before sunrise, no droving after sunset.' He was raising his brows at her interest, but he seemed pleased.

'I see.' Georgina *could* almost see, and she half-shut her eyes in pleasure. 'But why' ... and she opened her eyes again ... 'am I wanted?'

'Because I damn well know,' he grinned, 'that you wouldn't stay at home.' So he had seen her enchantment.

About to deny this, all at once Georgina was smiling back.

Cut it out, she told herself at once, and grin instead. Be offhand about it. Don't forget you're a man.

'So,' finished Roper, 'that's on our plates first.'

What was on the droving plate the next few days was beef and shepherd's pie.

'No brisket?' Georgina asked once.

'That's for geos who haven't time to lift their heads, and who are not within call of sympathetic pastoralists anxious to hand across something to keep body and soul together.' (This shepherd's pie had come, with a large pumpkin, from a beef farmer suffering the same worrying cattle slump as Roper's.) 'Droving, as you must have appreciated by now, is an entirely different story.'

Joanne, who had turned the shepherd's pie over and over with distaste and refused the pumpkin, averted her face. She hated every minute of the overlanding, and was often hard put to conceal her resentment from Roper. She certainly made no bones about it when the two girls were together.

'I can't last ten days, I can't!' she exclaimed.

'I think that it's important that you do.'

'Important for whom?' There was a sudden sly light in Joanne's eyes, something that Georgina was familiar with. It had always meant that Joanne was up to something.

'For you, I should say,' Georgina answered frankly, 'having pegged your claim on Mr Roper.'

'Speak your own language, George, you aren't a geologist, and never will be, yet I really think now you believe you are one.'

'Well, you know what I meant.'

'Oh, yes, I know, but——' again the crafty little light, 'but I'm tired,' Joanne finished pettishly.

'Tired in yourself or tired of the land?'

'Of the land. Horrible bare place that it is. Such boring colour!'

Georgina flushed. 'That's unfair, Joanne. There's colour to spare. The sunrises——'

'Which I'm forced to be up to see.'

'Well, the cattle have to be moved. Then the sunsets——'

'In civilised places,' broke in Joanne, 'people are drinking sundowners then. There is soft music, smooth waiters——'

'Oh, Joanne!' Georgina paused. 'Also when the light catches the rocks——'

'Now you're talking sense.'

'The light on the rocks?'

'The rocks themselves,' corrected Joanne, 'all with dollar signs on them, I hope.'

Georgina gave a little sigh but made no comment. Not that Joanne would have heard her, for she was thinking aloud.

'Yet you had something there when you asked me whether I was tired in myself or tired of the land. Come to think of it I *am* tired in myself.' Her eyes positively glinted with craft now. 'All this riding!'

'You're a good rider, Joanne.' That was true. Joanne had been indulged much more in riding, just as she had been indulged much more in everything. Not because either of their parents had wanted it that way, but because Joanne had seen to it that she got it. 'You look wonderful in your gear,' Georgina added, and Joanne nodded, impatient at being told something she already knew.

'Really, it's beginning to tell on me,' she said half to herself, half to Georgina. 'I've never been strong like you.'

'Joanne, you've had remarkably good health. Why, everyone always said——'

'Everyone is not me, *I* am me, so I should know.' Without another word Joanne turned on her heel, evidently seeking out Larry by the way she looked around her as she pulled her horse, Big Tim, behind her. Why can't she lead him, not tug him? wondered Georgina, but that, she knew, was like Joanne.

It was lucky for the mount that Larry was not far away. Georgina saw the mighty Roper get off Gibraltar, then the two of them, Joanne and Roper, strolled to a thicket of mulga safely clear of the beasts and away from the stock-

154

men—and from Georgina—then began to talk.

What was the conversation? Georgina thought, and she tried to ignore a stab of envy. For the talk out here had been magic to Georgina. There had been very little by day, they had been too busy then, but at night it had been all the wonderful stories of the west; cattle rustlers, poddy dodgers, stories learned from the aborigines of the Dreamtime. Bush songs, bush poetry. Clancy.

Biting her lip, Georgina turned away.

She was helping Sam with a stubborn beast some time later when Roper cut in.

'I want a word with you, George.'

'Yes, boss.' Out here Georgina had been calling him what all the stockmen called the head man on a drove— Boss. She turned her mount and cantered to where he had cantered, and now waited.

'Has Joanne been talking to you?' he asked at once.

'Well——' Georgina did not know what to say.

'Poor girl, I see she has. Don't be embarrassed, George. If she told me, surely as men we can discuss it. After all, there's nothing more agonising than saddle sores. She's been a brick to have lasted this long.'

'Saddle sores?' she echoed.

'Yes. You see, she has confided in me. You could see she hated doing it, but when you're in pain——'

'Yes, boss.'

'I expect she said a whole lot more to you, you being her stepbrother.' Roper looked inquiring.

'Well——'

'Well, she had to tell someone, poor child.' He was looking across at her; looking very hard, Georgina could feel the boring of his eyes again, but she could not trust herself to look back. That girl, she was thinking, that little liar Joanne! Joanne, she felt certain, had nothing of the sort. She recalled that little flick in Joanne's sweet, innocent eyes. Well, it seemed the ruse had paid off.

'We can't expect her to go any further,' Roper said.

'If you say so.'

'What do you mean by that?' Now he had narrowed the eyes. 'Do you doubt for a minute——'

'I only said if you say so because you're the boss,' cut in Georgina promptly.

'Well, as the boss I say just that,' he said firmly.

'What will you do with her then until we're ready to return? Make a permanent camp and leave her?'

'No, I don't like that idea. Once I might have, but now the world isn't quite such an innocent place as it was. There are undercurrents, subtleties, deceits.' It may have been her imagination, but Georgina thought he flicked her a glance at 'deceits'.

'Then how about some homestead?' she asked.

'Good lord, not for Joanne!'

'No,' agreed Georgina, 'she wouldn't even eat the shepherd's pie. I really mean——'

'I know exactly what you mean, Brown, and don't be so smug about it, because you're evidently a "natural" yourself. It's only to be expected of a man.'

'Yes, boss,' she said meekly.

'No, we'll send the little girl home.'

'Home?' she echoed.

'To Roper's.' He spoke impatiently. 'Those sores probably need attention. I've first aid naturally, but a woman likes to—well——' He broke off, and Georgina set her lips and did not help him.

Presently he said crisply:

'You will take her.'

'What?' she said, startled.

'You heard me, Brown.'

'Yes, I did, but——'

'Yes, Brown?' he asked inexorably.

'I don't want to go, sir.' There were a dozen things that Georgina could have babbled ... pleaded. The desert at sun-up, with so much gold you felt like King Midas, the desert at sundown, and indigo, violet, burnt sienna, ochre.

She hadn't heard the last of the poddy-dodger stories, either, the Dreamtime tales, the bush songs, the bush poetry. Clancy.

She looked at him piteously, forgetting she was a male. Then she remembered, and looked away.

'It has to be you, Brown. All the others are needed.' He said it a little more gently, if this man could be gentle. 'You've done well, but naturally since it isn't your job, not as well as they do. So you can be spared.'

'Why can't she' ... a look from Roper set Georgina correcting herself ... 'why can't Joanne go alone?'

'She's a woman.' He paused. 'Also she isn't so experienced as you are up here. You're a natural, as I said before. I'll have no qualms about sending you two back.'

'All that way——'

'As the track goes I'll agree its "all that way", but you will straighten out the curves of the track, a thing you can do when you're on a horse with no mob around you. Don't look alarmed, you can't possibly get lost.'

'It's still a long way,' she said miserably.

'Will you be surprised when I tell you that with "straightening out the track" you'll do it in a day?'

'Which day?' asked Georgina forlornly.

'Tomorrow. That girl can't wait any longer. Spare her as much as you can, Brown, but still don't dawdle. If you push off at first light you should make Roper's by five.' He was looking at her very closely now. 'Understood?'

'Understood,' Georgina said. 'Will you tell her or will I tell her?'

'I will tell Joanne,' he said coldly. 'When I was a youngster "her" or "she" was the cat's mother.'

'Still is.' Georgina said it to herself, not crediting he would hear. But he did, and his hand shot out and he whirled her and Ribbons round to him. The mount, who had been grazing, whinnied with surprise.

'Watch your tongue, Brown,' Roper said.

'Yes, sir.' Georgina stood very still until he took away his hand, then she escaped.

Later in the day a jubilant Joanne cantered across to her. If there were any saddle sores, thought Georgina, she was being very brave about them.

'It worked! I would have preferred a car to come out and fetch me, but at least I'll be away from this place.'

'I'm to conduct you,' Georgina said.

'Yes, and see you do it efficiently or the big boss will have something to say.' Joanne smiled and she looked like the kitten who had got the cream. '*Handle with care*. You can see it in his eyes.'

'I can't,' retorted Georgina.

'Of course you can't, the care is for me, not you. You'd better get me back safely.'

'For whom?' The words seemed to say themselves, and Georgina looked uneasily at Joanne.

Joanne looked back at her with narrowed eyes.

'You're getting a bit too smart, George.' Joanne was supreme mistress of the situation. 'Just get me back without any comment. Oh, dear, it's going to be a bore getting up at first light.'

'You've done it all this week.'

'Second light,' corrected Joanne blandly. 'I always had a cuppa brought to me. Did you? But then you're George.' She laughed as Georgina cantered away.

They were sent to their sleeping bags early that night, no disappointment for Joanne, for the campfire talk bored her, but Georgina fretted with disappointment.

She lay awake watching the fire flicker through the bush that separated the camp from the sleeping bags, listening to the men's voices but not being able to hear the words. She decided she had better sleep if she wanted to do a good job tomorrow, and began counting stars in the hope of slipping off. The campfire had been stamped out, and the men had gone to their sleeping bags ... with the exception of the herd watchers ... before she did lose consciousness.

Some time later she woke up, and she wondered whether

the snores to left and right had done it, though they hadn't disturbed her on other nights.

Then faintly yet clearly she heard it; someone singing the cattle. Singing the cattle was always done when one of the beasts was restless, but it hadn't been needed yet on this drove. But someone was singing now. The song was *Always*. I'll be loving you always.

. . . I'm all for always. Are you?

It was Larry Roper singing. Singing to the cattle. And to Joanne.

Georgina was not conscious of crying, but she must have been, for when Roper called at first light: 'Rise and shine!' her face felt stiff, and touching it she recognised the roughness of salt. She sluiced herself quickly, drank down the scalding tea she was handed so fast that Roper's eyebrows shot up, then on Ribbons, with a yawning Joanne on Big Tim, she left the overlanders and started for home.

Joanne grumbled all the way and all the day, but apart from her complaining voice it wasn't at all bad. Larry Roper had been right about "straightening the track". Years of droving the cattle over it had given it unnecessary curves and bends, but by detouring into the scrub, though always keeping the road in view, you cut off miles.

By four o'clock in the afternoon they were approaching the Roper station.

'I can't get to that bath quick enough,' said Joanne.

'Want me to help you with any dressings?' asked Georgina.

Joanne gave her a pitying look. 'Don't be an ass,' she said. 'No, there's nothing a hot wallow won't fix. I'm going to lie in and soak and soak. I'm going to use up every drop of hot water.—No. No, I'm not.' Suddenly, so suddenly that Georgina could think of nothing to say, Joanne turned round and smiled radiantly at her.

'No, I'm not,' she repeated. Then she announced: '*You* are.'

'I'm what?' Georgina was taken aback.

'You've been wonderful, and I do appreciate it. You're going to have first go of the bath, and don't dare budge from it for an hour.'

'But, Joanne——'

'You've done twice the riding I have.' That was true, Georgina had checked each short cut first. 'You've really deserved what you're getting, Georgina.' *Georgina* not George, 'and that is first go. No, no, I insist.'

Mollified—well, she had to feel mollified—Georgina stammered her objections, then, when pressed again, her thanks.

It was wonderful, she appreciated an hour later, to lie and soak. She shut her eyes in the relaxation of it all. How kind Joanne had been, how unexpectedly kind. It made it all the better when you hadn't anticipated anything like that.

At last she dragged herself out, mopped herself dry with Willy's fluffy white towels, and got into some crisp jeans and a shirt that Joanne had insisted on providing for her, and that Georgina had decided should be safe on this occasion, seeing there were no men about.

Willy was there, of course, but Willy's attention as usual was on other things, mainly Joanne.

'Milady's not here,' she told Georgina when Georgina, scrubbed and refreshed went into the kitchen, 'she went out as she was, all stained and dirty. Not like a princess. There's something doing, if you ask me.'

'Did she go out to the road?' Surely Joanne had not gone looking for Craig, dishevelled after a day's ride; that didn't sound like Joanne at all.

'She just went out and got in her car and went down your track,' replied Willy.

'To the hut?'

'Yes, George. Ah, here she is now.'

Perhaps, thought Georgina, watching Joanne pull up at the homestead steps, poor Joanne couldn't stand being dirty any longer, so had gone and had a bath in the basin rather than hurry me up. In Joanne's present wonderful mood she might do that.

But Joanne was still dishevelled. She was also a little excited, but Georgina did not take any notice of that.

'Finished?' Joanne asked. 'Then I'm for it.' She went along to the bathroom, and Georgina did not see any more of her that evening.

She had a cup of tea with Willy, then, pleading tiredness, she refused dinner, saying she would have an early night.

It was dark when she reached her hut, but the kerosene lamp soon saw to that. She looked at the little room fondly. I believe I've come to love it, she thought. It was masculinely sparse, deliberately so on Georgina's part, for every woman can add a female touch. But its neatness pleased her, and she frowned slightly over her report papers that were not stacked as she should have stacked them. She must have gone out in a hurry. She tidied them now.

Mrs Willmott's tea had taken any edge away from her appetite, but bed called.

She decided to turn in at once; after all, she had not slept well last night. She had watched the camp-fire, listened to the men's voices; she had heard someone singing the cattle. Larry had, and the song had been 'Always'. I'll be loving you always. *'I'm all for always. Are you?'*

'Yes. Yes, Larry.'

Georgina said it, but she did not know she said it. She was asleep.

CHAPTER THIRTEEN

SOMETHING had happened to Joanne. She was so nice to
Georgina that Georgina should have been suspicious, but,
just as when she had been growing up, Georgina melted
again at a kind word from her stepsister. There had never
been many kind words, in fact only when Joanne wanted
something, but it made no difference to Georgina now. She
reacted at once, and warmly. I guess you could say, she told
herself in one of her clearer moments, that I'm just a sucker
for love. Always she had wanted to be friends with Joanne;
she had yearned for closeness, for confidences, for 'girls
together', for affection without competition, and now that
Joanne offered all these she accepted them gladly.

'You're being so nice, Joanne.' Georgina simply could
not help saying that.

'Well, it came to me very forcibly on that ride home how
awfully sweet you are, Georgina. I'm afraid it's taken me a
long time to find out.' Joanne hung her head. 'But that's
Joanne for you. Spoiled, a real brat.'

'Oh, no!'

'Well, thank you, darling, for denying it. I must say it's
lovely having a sister instead of a stepsister.' Joanne actually caught Georgina's hand and pressed it, then she kissed
her—the first time, Georgina realised, they had kissed in
their lives. Even when Stepfather had brought his daughter
to meet her, and Mother had pushed her own daughter to
meet Joanne, there had only been blank stares. Oh,
Georgina had been ready with her love, over-ready. That
had been, and was, a bad point in her really, she had too
much love. But when Joanne had repulsed her she had

caught on quickly, and been quite as adept as Joanne at poking out a hating tongue the moment the adults' backs had been turned.

But now everything was different. Joanne slipped her arm in Georgina's. She came down to the hut every day; she was a changed girl.

She was determined to help Georgina, and though Georgina could have done without that help, Joanne's disappointed face undid her, and she allowed Joanne to take over the typing.

'But only until Mr Roper comes back, Jo. My goodness, what would he think of me giving my work out like this?'

'Oh, yes, I wouldn't do it then,' Joanne agreed.

She became intensely interested in the rocks. She even begged Georgina to let her stay with her whenever Georgina worked on their samples. As Larry Roper had shown her the lab previously, Georgina saw no harm in it, and was rewarded with Joanne's rapt (if un-understanding) pretty face. The mighty Roper, thought Georgina a little sadly, is going to get more than he thinks, for Joanne is quite absorbed in it all, naïvely so, but nonetheless gratifyingly interested.

'What are those ducky coloured ribbons?' Joanne asked childishly.

'They do the same as flags do in offices, Jo, they show where the action is—or, in this case, where it will be.'

Joanne clapped her hands. 'It's quite thrilling, and they do look pretty.'

She was sweet and innocent and Georgina's heart went out to her. After all, she had lost a parent all those years ago just as the young Georgina had. It was simply a case of different reactions to a bereavement that Joanne had had animosity in her all these years. Now it was a thing of the past.

The girls really enjoyed themselves; the only flaw in that week before Larry Roper returned was the loss of the lab key. But barely had the loss been discovered than the key turned up again, so everything was all right.

All right, that was, as far as Joanne and Georgina were concerned. When the thought of Larry Roper intruded, it was a different story for Georgina. She wondered how Joanne felt. Perhaps—and Georgina felt a sharp stab—it was because of Larry that Joanne had changed like this. Love did change people. Well, it was a good thing, a wonderful thing, but——

The next evening the first roster of overlanders returned.

The second relief had left previously, taking more supplies as well as more stock. For more babies had been born during the week, and being four-footed and able to run within hours, they travelled, too.

The baths ran hot and long that first night. After that food was next on the list, food as Willy or Cooky presented it, for though they had been well fed on the track, there had been no frills, and no pudding. It was amazing how these big, tough cattlemen looked for sweets.

Roper came down to the hut after he had soaked and scrubbed. He was now, he told Georgina, a different colour. Also, he grinned, the bath was as well.

'Yes, I know,' laughed Georgina. 'It happened to me.'

'Don't tell me that Joanne allowed you in the bath, George! Oh, I know she would eventually, but not that first night.'

'That first night,' confirmed Georgina. 'What's more, I was the first.'

'You amaze me. So does Joanne. Well, Brown, are you ready to push off?'

'On the check-ups?'

'Where else?' he inquired.

'Of course I'm ready, but aren't you tired?'

'Not tired, but even if I were I'd still go. You don't postpone things like these' ... he waved an arm to Georgina's table of papers ...'and already too much time has been lost. We'll leave tomorrow. It'll be a brief trip, just that double check, no new exploration. No need for any change of clothes, no need for anything but sleeping bags and tucker. We'll do it tough.'

'Yes, Mr Roper.'

It occurred to Georgina that the new Joanne might like to come, and she asked Larry Roper.

'She was all against it before,' he said, 'she couldn't even last out the overland.'

'She's different now,' she averred.

'How different?' He looked at her keenly.

'She's—co-operative. She's nice. I thought it must be——' Georgina broke off.

'Yes, George?'

'Love. She's a changed person.'

'Interesting,' he said. 'All right, you can ask her.'

'I thought it should come from you.'

'If it came from me it would come falsely, Brown. I don't want her. I don't want any females on this trip.'

'No,' gulped Georgina, 'but——'

'Oh, yes, I agree with you she would look very pretty under the stars of a night, but by that time I—and you— will be so dead beat we'll have hit the hay, crawled into our sleeping bags and be lost to the world. It's strictly business this time, but if you like, mention it to Joanne.'

Georgina did, and for the briefest of moments Joanne's eyes narrowed thoughfully. But it was quite infinitesimal, the next instant Joanne was saying: 'What a lovely thought, but I know it's only going to be a rush trip, Georgina, and I would be in the way. I wouldn't want to be but it would happen, me being silly little me, and Larry would be irritated.'

'So you won't come?'

'Invitation declined regretfully. Perhaps some other time——' Joanne gave yet another of the sweet smiles she flung around like so much largesse these days.

Roper and Brown—Larry had laughingly tagged them that—left early the following morning. Larry drove the jeep and Georgina sat with her map and compass and kept her eyes peeled for their marking ribbons.

Everything went well. They had checked more than half of their estimated 'signs' by the end of the day.

Dinner was the same iron ration as last time, brisket on bread, and bed came the minute night descended.

The following morning they did so well with their checks that they could have turned round and made for Roper's and arrived there, work completed, by night. But something stopped them. It could have been the herby tang of the desert, the quiet that you could almost feel, the inverted blue bowl of sky, the warm gold sun ... it could have been anything, but somehow neither of them was inclined to turn back. It was purely instinctive, and it happened to both of them.

Georgina did try weakly with the reminder to Roper that he had wanted to waste no time over the claims, but the prompting was taken as weakly as it was given. The west had entrapped them both.

They just wasted time for the rest of the day, examining the bush, trying to remain as still as a gecko lizard, looking for the occasional smooth lucky stone among the sharp gibber, sometimes just drowsing on sun-warmed rocks.

Then it was brisket and bread and the sleeping bags again, but this time, because their work was over, they had a moment to talk before they slept.

Georgina told Larry how mirages had always fascinated her, and how her stepfather had believed that water scenes being enacted elsewhere were created a second time, as in a mirror, and that it wasn't just imagination on your part as some people believed.

'I can back him up on that,' agreed Larry Roper, 'I saw something once that had been repeated faithfully.'

'What was it?'

He did not answer.

'Sir?'

'You're too young, Brown.' Georgina could not see Roper,

but she had a suspicion that he was grinning.

She left that subject and told him that her only regret so far up here had been her very restricted view of the fabled Lucy.

'I only saw an anabranch before,' she reminded him, 'but I would have liked to have looked across its sixty miles.'

He grunted. 'That would be a long look, Brown. Anyway, it's not sixty now, more like a mere thirty, and still dwindling.'

'Yet I would have liked to have looked.' Georgina could not help adding that.

'Persistent boy, aren't you? Very well then, tomorrow.'

'Tomorrow? But——'

'But I want to get back? Yes, Brown, I do. But as it happens I want to look, too. Goodnight, George.'

'Goodnight, boss.'

The next day, the charts put away now but the compass left out, they set straight through the bush in a north-west direction which Roper said should bring them to the main wide section of the strange river. Big River Country. Again Georgina heard Stepfather telling her about it, telling of its greatness and its lowliness, its eternal mysticism. Her excitement grew.

The Lucy did not let her down. They rounded a clump of sage and there it shimmered as far as the eye could reach. It was the bluest bluebell blue that Georgina had ever seen.

Forgetting she was supposed to be a male, she clapped her hands at it, ran down to its edge to look closer at it, to put in a toe. This then was the fabled river that dwindled to a trickle, sometimes disappeared altogether, but now it was a weaving expanse of water. Gulls flew over it. There were even waves crashing to the shore.

They spent the day there, with no thought of returning now. They explored the beachy edge, and even found a variety of crab. It was weird and wonderful, but most of all it was beautiful. More beautiful than Georgina could have dreamed.

'Thank you, Larry.' In her pleasure she did not hear herself say his name. If he noticed, he gave no sign.

They camped by the river, and every time Georgina woke that night she heard the waterbells of the Big Lucy. I think, she said a little deliriously to herself, I have never been happier in my life; I don't know why, but I am.

The next morning they knew they really must start back, so after breakfast—bread, brisket and tea again—they set the jeep eastwards once more.

It was not until mid-morning that Roper stopped the waggon and said: 'Trouble.'

'The engine?' Georgina asked.

'No, thank heaven. It's not our transport that's letting us down, it's the direction.'

'Have I read wrongly?'

'You've read it very well, George, but something has happened. Something like an upside-down creek that's decided to right itself at the wrong moment. Do you recall a sticky patch yesterday?'

'Yes,' she said promptly.

'That,' and now Georgina noticed quite a large creek in front of them, 'is the patch.'

'It couldn't be!' she exclaimed.

'Yes it is.'

'It didn't rain last night.'

'That's nothing to do with it, Brown. Somewhere it rained some time ago, and last night the water hit here, and our sticky patch, fed underground, changed to this creek.'

'Oh, no!'

'Oh, yes, unfortunately for us. I have a good eye for water, and I believe when I check, which is going to be now, that that creek is going to be too deep for us to cross.' He had got out and gone down to the creek edge, and as Georgina watched, he walked in. He was right about the level. It was not deep for _him_, but it was too deep for a jeep, even a special bush waggon made for contingencies like these.

168

'What do we do?' asked Georgina, vexed with herself, for if she hadn't expressed a wish to see the river this wouldn't have happened. 'Do we wait till it goes down again?'

'That could take days. No, I'll have to find another route.'

'I'll help you.'

'You'll stay in the jeep, Brown. That's an order,' he said harshly.

'I don't blame you,' said Georgina sensitively, 'I have messed things up.'

He looked at her and shook his head. 'I'm angry,' he admitted, 'but perish the thought that I'm angry with you. I wanted to go to the Lucy, too. It's just bad luck that this has happened at this precise moment. Ordinarily a wait here could be pleasurable with the right companion, and you're a right one, Brown, but just now——' He frowned.

He repeated his command that she stayed by the jeep, then he took the compass and started to scout around for a possible detour. While he was away Georgina got a fire going so that the billy was boiling when he returned.

He was glad of the tea, but he had no glad news. The creek still stopped them from crossing, he reported, yet cross they must if they were to get back.

'One thing,' said Georgina, 'we can't die of thirst.'

'If that's supposed to be clever——' he snapped.

'It wasn't, sir. I'm sorry.'

'It's all right, Brown. I'm a bit touchy. To be held up by that apology—well, it is an apology after the Lucy—for a string of water.'

'Perhaps if you try the other direction——'

'Yes, I will. You stay put, as I said. Without the jeep we won't be any good.'

This time he was gone longer than before, which Georgina decided might be good news. He must have found a patch that the waggon could manage, but, typical of Roper, he was double-checking first, just as he had with the nickel.

Georgina sat and waited.

The time went on; she estimated it was early afternoon now. She closed her eyes for a moment, or so she intended, then half slept, but it must have been half-sleep, for the shadow across her semi-shut lids sent her eyes opening widely. At first she could see nothing unusual, it was just the same as before; then, in the shadow of a rock, she saw a man. On ochre-coloured man, naked except for a loin-cloth, and he was watching her.

Georgina got up and put out her hand to him. He did not come, yet he did not go away. She wondered if there was a tribe with him; there were few tribes left now in the west, they had gone to the towns and the missions, but some of the aboriginals still travelled the desert, still lived as their forefathers had lived.

He looked quite splendid standing there, a straight spare figure carved in dark red ochre. Possibly, yet not probably, he had never seen a white person before. Most certainly he would not have met many.

She went towards him, hand still out, speaking to him, though she knew that if he had had no white contact he would not understand a word. He was not afraid of her, though, and she was unafraid of him. The dark eyes, black eyes with a touch of red somewhere in them, were extra-ordinarily gentle. But then they were a very gentle people, she knew.

She came up to him and smiled, but he did not smile back. He took a few steps away from her now, then he turned and beckoned her with quiet eyes. That was all Georgina could have called it, a beckoning.

She went across. As soon as she reached him, he moved again, beckoned with his eyes again. This happened four times, then after that Georgina got the message. He wanted to take her somewhere, and she had a fair idea why. Larry must have come to some mishap, she thought, and the native had seen him and come, or been told to come, to fetch her.

All at once the terrain altered. It had been flat ever since they left the Lucy, but abruptly the creek that the man and Georgina had followed disappeared underground again, leaving a narrow crossing, squelchy-looking and actually with algae growing in places, but still negotiable, Georgina judged. So where was Larry?

She looked to the aborigine, and he did the beckoning act again, so she followed and saw what had happened. A narrow cleft opened up no more than ten yards from the possible crossing, opened up without any warning. At the bottom of the cleft, not deep but certainly deep enough to inflict an injury, lay the mighty Roper. He must have been looking around to see if there were any other ways through without the squelch and mud, in his absorption not looked where he was going, and dropped suddenly, just as that drop of water from a rock at the top was dropping now.

Georgina did not waste a moment; she leapt, then slid down the cleft.

Larry was lying quite straight, thank heaven, no fear from entwined arms or twisted legs. In fact everything about him seemed quite normal.

She leaned over and regarded him, then she edged his head on to her lap. What should she do? Go back for the first-aid kit? Yet what did she have in the kit that he needed? There appeared to be nothing broken, nothing cut.

What about mouth-to-mouth respiration? That, she knew, was the only obvious treatment. She took a deep preparatory breath, then leaned over.

'Oh, no, Brown.' His voice came clearly up to her. 'I'd like that as much from you as you'd like it from me. Now if you were a girl instead——'

'You—you are all right?' she asked, startled.

'A bit knocked out, that's all,' he responded.

'Why didn't you let me know?' Relief brought a querulous note to Georgina's voice. 'Why, I might have—I might——'

'That's why I did let you know just now,' he grinned, and

171

added: 'In the nick of time.'

'If this is your idea of a joke——'

'It's not. I *was* knocked out. A good winding, as I had, is as bad as a thump on the skull. But your intent look brought me to, quick-smart.'

'You're unspeakable!'

'Then don't speak.' He shut his eyes, and she wriggled his head from her lap on to the ground and waited for him to recover fully. He did so quite soon.

'Your lap was more comfortable that the hard earth,' he said feelingly, 'even though I would prefer more padding. What a pity you're George, George Brown; girls are much more accommodating.'

She did not comment on that. She looked around for their Adam in ochre, but could not see him.

'No,' said Larry, following her look, 'he'll be gone.'

'Can't we find him? Thank him?'

'He wouldn't understand that, I mean he wouldn't comprehend a need for thanks. It was simply something that had to be done.'

'Did he show you the way across?' Georgina asked.

'No, I found that myself, but I knew he was watching. He had been watching when we arrived. He followed me here. I knew as I fell that it would be all right, that he would find and bring you.'

'But he wouldn't know where I was,' she protested.

'They always know.'

'Where has he gone?'

'Probably to his tribe. There are very few single nomads. Thank heaven for them all, anyway. This could have been tricky, George.' Roper had got to his feet now, and Georgina saw that he swayed a little before he could steady himself enough to climb out of the cleft. He must have felt her eyes on him, for he said sharply: 'I'm all right.'

'Of course,' she agreed.

They walked back to the jeep, and all the way Georgina watched him obliquely. He was not as well as he was trying to make out he was, she thought: he spoke normally, though, as he said their dark friend would be far away by this, as they would be, too, very soon.

'How far away?' Georgina asked.

'Home,' he said simply.

'Roper's?'

'Where else is home?'

'But I thought we were a long way off,' she protested.

'Once we're on the other side of the creek, as we can be now, we should make it by sunset. You see we'll be cutting off a great hunk of terrain with this detour. You'll be navigating, Brown.'

'Yes, sir.'

They wasted no time in leaving. Roper concentrated on the task of crossing the mud, but it caused only a little trouble. Some canvas under the wheel and a push and they were on firm ground.

Navigating, too, was no worry. Roper told Georgina what he wanted and she was able to give clear directions; in fact the only concern was the driver. Taking care not to let him see her checking, Georgina noted that Roper was tiring. When he made several poor judgments, such as failing to detour over gibber patches, not avoiding a tree until it was almost too late, she looked at him more openly. His eyelids were drooping, his mouth was slack. He had a late reaction, she knew. But she could not take over both the driving and the navigation as well, so she let him fumble along until she saw a first landmark, one of the bores of the outer edge of Roper's, a long distance from the homestead, but she knew she could find her way from here.

She spoke quietly but firmly to the man, and told him to stop. While he still fumbled on, she knew he hadn't heard her, he was beyond that, and he was driving as an automaton might have driven. So Georgina put out her hand and braked the jeep herself, then she killed the engine. She got out and came round to the driver's seat and edged Larry gently into her seat. He didn't resist; in fact by the time

173

she found something to put at the back of his head, he was asleep.

She was unfamiliar with a four-wheel drive, but mechanics had never been a trouble to her. By trial and error she soon found out about it and thirty minutes later she was pulling up at the homestead, shouting out to Mrs Willmott to contact the flying doctor, calling for help from the men to get Roper to bed.

The doctor was there very promptly. He said: 'You again!' to Georgina, and: 'This is becoming a habit' to a hovering Mrs Willmott.

As he examined the patient he told Georgina wryly that the two of them, Roper and Brown, must be a bad combination. 'I'd never been called to attend the mighty Roper, but now you've come I've had two calls in a month. The same as last time: Just watch him and he'll come round. Can you do that?'

'Oh, yes,' Georgina assured him. 'There's Mrs Willmott, and I'll watch after I've cleaned up, and there's Joanne.'

From the other side of the bed Willy said: 'There isn't. She's left.'

'Left?' The doctor had gone out to fetch something, but it would have been all the same if he had been there. Georgina could not have contained herself. 'When?' she said incredulously.

'The day that you left.'

'Then she's been gone a week?'

'That's right,' Mrs Willmott nodded.

'But she's coming back.' Georgina looked down at Larry Roper. 'She must be coming back. I mean——'

'She's gone. All her things are gone—her clothes, her car, everything. I would say, George, that your stepsister has definitely moved on.'

174

CHAPTER FOURTEEN

LEFT. Gone. Moved on.

At first Georgina could not get that fact into her muddled head. Mrs Willmott was being fanciful; she never had liked her stepsister and it was just something to say. Why, Joanne never would have moved on, she had too much at stake here. She had Larry Roper—she had Roper's.

That Joanne would abandon Larry, Georgina might have believed eventually; Joanne had gone through strings of men before in her young life. But abandoning money, for Roper's represented that, was harder to accept. That was unless Joanne had found someone else with more money, or the prospect of more, but who was there out here? And it would have to be someone out here, for Joanne had not been in touch with Sydney for weeks. She had said once to Georgina: 'I've turned that page for a new page, let's hope there's something more interesting in the print.'

Mrs Willmott was babbling on, but softly, keeping her voice down because of Larry.

Because of Larry. Georgina looked down at the man and felt very near to tears. She did not know how things really had been between him and her stepsister, but she did know that even if Larry Roper would not be hurt then his pride would certainly be toppled. A man's pride was a very real thing, so Georgina suffered for Larry Roper.

'A good riddance, if you ask me,' Willy was mumbling. 'Always out in that little car of hers "looking at the country". But a lot of country looking she did.' Willy sniffed. 'No,' she went on, 'she met *him*.'

'Who, Mrs Willmot?'

'That fellow Craig Everson. He caused enough trouble here before, and now he's caused it again.'

You really mean, Georgina interpreted miserably to herself, that he robbed the mighty Roper of four girls, and now it will be five.

'If you ask me——' began Willy again, but she stopped as she saw the doctor signalling her from the door. 'Pumpkin scones,' she sighed, but not without pride, and went out.

'If you ask me,' said Larry Roper clearly from the sick bed, 'I've been got at.' He looked up at Georgina and grinned, a grin that soon stretched to a laugh. Then they both laughed.

'You don't sound heartbroken,' Georgina said.

'I'm not. It never was like that with your stepsister, George. What in heaven gave you such a rum idea?'

Georgina hesitated. 'Joanne, I suppose. She—was—well——'

'Possessive? I've had possessive females before Joanne, but it never came to anything.'

'Because they left you as Joanne has?'

'Because I prefer a different type,' he returned.

'Retiring, you mean?'

'Something like that. Someone who's encased in a shell.'

'But then you would never see it ... see her,' she stumbled.

'But I would know she was there,' he replied.

There was a pause.

'Then your pride isn't toppled?' asked Georgina.

'Oh, for heaven's sake, boy, no! The girl came here, I extended the usual western hospitality to her, and there it ends.' He closed his eyes.

But it didn't end, though it didn't occur to either of them then. Georgina was the first to make the discovery.

She had brought Larry straight to the homestead, and now, since he needed no watching, she went down at last to her hut. The moment she stepped inside the room, she knew.

'Oh, no!' she cried.

The room itself was untouched, but her desk was in a turmoil. The papers had been turned over, those not needed ... like her notes for the book ... tossed carelessly on the floor. But everything to do with the exploration—not the exploration in the Roper property but beyond the property, the fields where they had found the really big signs and consequently double-checked—was gone.

Georgina went through all the papers again—she must have made a mistake! But she hadn't. All the pertinent details were missing, and only the non-relevant notes remained.

She sat down and bit by bit she began to piece things together.

That day she and Joanne had come back from the drove and Joanne had generously insisted that Georgina have first bath, when she had come down to her hut later she had had a feeling she had not left her papers quite like that. Now it wasn't just a feeling, she *knew*. While she had been up at the homestead, Joanne had come and taken what she needed to take. Whether that had been the beginning, she did not know, but she did know now that other things had followed.

Joanne suddenly becoming a different person, Joanne pleading to type for her. A lost lab key. It had only been lost for a short period, but in that period Joanne could have had a duplicate cut; this was remote country, but she still might have known where to go.

Had she had a duplicate cut? There was only one way to find out. Georgina went up to the house.

She went straight to the lab and put her own key in the door. But she did not turn the key, for there was no need. Someone in the lab must have heard her coming.

Larry Roper opened the door.

'Yes,' he said to her unasked question, and his voice was

tired, discouraged, 'we're a week too late. Well,' stepping back for Georgina to come right in, 'what do you think?'

What did she think? Georgina looked around and knew a moment of truth which, at another quick look at his tired and discouraged face, he must have known too, and only minutes before, for all the signs of shock and dismay remained.

Like the end of the table where she had done her reports, the pertinent portion of the lab was in a shambles. Everything to do with what they had discovered was missing.

'She evidently knew, or was told, what to take, because——' Larry shrugged helplessly and extended his hands.

'Joanne wouldn't know, she would have to be told. But who?' Yet even as she said it, Georgina's voice trailed off. There was only one possible person.

'She came from Sydney with this idea?' Roper asked.

'Oh, no, she wouldn't know about it then.'

He did not speak, but he was looking at her keenly.

Gulping, Georgina said: 'Would—Craig Everson— would he——'

'Yes, he would,' Roper said grimly, 'He'd do anything to settle a score with me.'

'But it's more than that, isn't it? It was something bigger than a settled score he was after. But would he have that knowledge?'

'Everyone out here has a bit of know-how. Why, even Willy knows rocks from scones. Wouldn't you, with a possible million waiting to be unearthed? But apart from that Everson would know very clearly. He might not have made a raging success at being a pastoralist, but he was always a bright boy.'

'It needn't have been him,' Georgina said.

'I think you know, as I know, now, that it's him. They met at Fortescues', didn't they? Oh, yes, I saw them in my headlights just as you did. I think they met pretty fre-

178

quently after that.'

'They did,' said Georgina.

'Why do you say that?' he demanded.

'My stepsister told me.'

'She told you, yet you saw no reason to pass the information on to me?'

'No. I was upset. I knew it wasn't right, but—but I didn't want you hurt.'

'What?' he rapped.

'At the time I thought—I believed——'

'Then you were, and are, a fool, Brown. But now your foolishness has gone a step further—You're a disaster. A disaster to me. Your consideration ... I can think of other words, but I won't use them ... has cost me a cool million. Yes,' at her stunned look, 'it has.'

She rallied. 'I'm not questioning the amount. I'm questioning the result of my consideration for you, as you put it. Surely there's time yet—surely they couldn't have——'

'I've been in touch with Mining H.Q. already.' Now Larry Roper paused, and when he spoke again he did so almost indifferently. 'I'm a week too late.'

'A week!'

'Seven days. The length of time we've been away. Our friends got to work at once. I think if we could question Joanne she would admit that she was in this lab five minutes after we took off, down at your hut ten minutes later. She wouldn't need long; she would have been well briefed as to what she was after.'

'And then?' Georgina questioned.

'Mrs Willmott provided the "and then". What was it she said while I lay concussed?' A wry laugh.

'She said,' said Georgina wretchedly, 'left ... gone ... moved on. But it takes a few days to get to Sydney by car, and by the time one settles in——' She stopped at the look on Roper's face.

'You little fool,' he said, 'if you went up to Brydens' now

179

you'd find two cars, Everson's and Joanne's. With a prospect as big as this, they would fly.'

'But there's no service from here.'

'They would charter a service with a million in view.'

'Do you really credit that sum?' she asked, awed.

'I know it,' he retorted.

'Do you really think they went straight to the Mines Department?'

'I also know that,' he said grimly, 'I told you so before. We're a week too late. The claims were registered and paid seven days ago. Well, it was a nice thought to be that rich. And at least it will keep her out of her stepbrother's hair, won't it?' He laughed sourly.

'It's all my fault.' Georgina stood and clasped and unclasped her hands. She waited a little piteously for him to say, 'No. No, it's one of those things,' but factually, baldly, a little cruelly, Roper agreed.

'Yes.'

There was a moment's silence in the verandah room that he had turned into a study-lab.

'You knew something was going on but you never told me, and don't go giving me that sentimental rot about not wanting to hurt me, because it doesn't ring true. Why didn't you tell me, Brown?'

Georgina shrugged. 'Because Joanne has always been like that, going through strings of men, I mean. She will probably tire of Craig.'

'Not with a fortune she won't. But *Craig*, you said—you sound knowledgable. Did you know him before?'

'I travelled up here with him. My outfit broke down halfway and Craig brought me the rest of the way.'

'That would give you several days and nights on the road,' he said sharply.

'Yes,' she admitted.

'So on your stepsister's arrival you promptly introduced the pair. Why?'

'I didn't. Craig saw Joanne one day—I was there, too—

180

then you and Joanne went past in your car, and he—well, he was instantly attracted. When Joanne came home she was interested too.'

'It went on from there?' he demanded.

'Yes.'

'And when did this' ... he spread his hands to the shambles ... 'first begin?'

'I don't know. I mean, I do now, but there were no signs then.'

'With him meeting her every day!'

'But that was typical of Joanne,' she pointed out.

'It was also typical of Everson. Did you know that from your journey up?' Again that sharp, probing note in his voice, but he did not probe. Instead he said: 'So you don't know when it began, but tell me what you do know, please.'

'Coming home from the overlanding, Joanne changed.'

'Yes, you mentioned that,' he agreed, 'she insisted you bathed first.'

'When I went to the hut I had the feeling something had been touched, not obviously like this, but—but——'

'Go on.'

'There wasn't anything else except Joanne insisting on typing for me.'

'What?' he demanded.

'Yes,' said Georgina miserably, 'and the key.'

'I was waiting for that,' he nodded.

'It was lost for a while. Only a short time.'

'But enough time for an impression to be made,' he said grimly.

'Yes,' Georgina agreed.

'Anything more? I mean, how did she know what was in there?'

'I—I'd taken her. She asked me to, and I saw no harm. All she did was clap her hands at the ribbons.'

'And now she's clapping her hands over our claims.'

'Your claims, Mr Roper. And I'm sorry.'

'I'm sorry, too. I've enough money, but a man is always

181

sufficiently ambitious to be interested in more, otherwise the world wouldn't go round. Besides' ... a pause ... 'I intend becoming a family man, and that always entails more.'

'You—are marrying?' she gasped.

'Yes.'

'Then Joanne wouldn't have——'

'Wouldn't have had a chance? No,' he agreed, tight-lipped.

'Congratulations, Mr Roper. Do I know her?' Georgina was trying to think of all the girls around, but then the chosen one might be a city girl, and possibly was. Mrs Willmott had said she believed there was someone, but she did not know where.

'Know her?' Roper said smoothly. 'No—no, I don't think you do, not a boy like you.'

'Mr Roper, I'll resign, of course,' she said with difficulty.

'Yes, I think so, Brown. After all, we can't go on like this.'

'Like what?' Georgina caught her breath and waited.

'Living in deceit as you have,' he returned.

'Deceit ...?' her voice faded away.

'Pretending all was well with Joanne when all the time she was——'

'Oh, that,' Georgina broke in.

'What else is there?' His glance was keen.

'Nothing, sir. If—if you've finished with me, sir, I'll go and pack.'

'By all means, George. I've finished with you.— George——' he said as Georgina reached the door.

'Yes, Mr Roper?' she hesitated.

'If you've anything else to say I'll still be here. At least I have to get back some order.'

About to offer to do it, Georgina said instead: 'What else do you want me to say?'

'The whole truth?' he suggested.

'You've had it.'

'Have I, Brown?'

She squared her shoulders. 'If you think you haven't, then it's up to you, isn't it, sir? Up to you, I mean, to reach your own conclusion.'

'It would still have to be *said*.' The mighty Roper began discarding sheets of now unwanted papers and throwing them into a basket.

Georgina went out.

She did not know how to get away from this place, for she had no transport and no Craig any longer to take her, and it was scarcely a road where you could stand and thumb a lift. Nonetheless Georgina packed and stacked and tried not to think. Whatever happens, even if I have to walk every step of the way with my haversack on my back, she thought, I will *not* go in and ask him for help to get away.

She did it like that. She left the bags as she had before and just took her essentials, then she went out of the little hut for ever, trudged up the track for the last time and began the long walk to the gate. Heaven only knew what would happen then.

She was still a long way from the gate when he came after her in the jeep.

'You damn fool, Brown, you can't think of walking, and your chances of a lift in a car are very remote.'

'I'll walk, and I'll camp at night,' she said defiantly.

'The heck you will! Haven't you ever heard of the dangers of the open road these days?'

'I can cope.'

'Even a man is hard put to cope, and you are only a——'

'Yes, Mr Roper?'

'Only a boy,' he finished.

She flushed. 'I don't want to borrow any transport, I don't know when I can return it.'

'Then the obvious thing is to keep working until you have enough money to enable you to leave independently.'

'But you don't want me, sir, you said so.'

'Yes, I did,' he said sternly, 'I've finished with George Brown.'

'Then——'

'Oh, no, Brown,' he smiled thinly, 'you're not tricking me into this. *You* have to say it.'

'Say what?'

'The whole truth. I told you so.'

'But I've given it all to you,' she said desperately, 'I've said how Craig and Joanne——'

'But you've still never said the most important thing, and it has to be said.'

'You mean—about me?' she asked faintly.

'Yes.' His smile was gone now.

'But why——'

'Because it has to be said. Because you have to come to me as a—— Good lord, George, I've known from the beginning! Is it that hard to tell me?'

'Yes. Yes, it is.'

'But why?'

'Because—well, because I'm brown and freckled and khaki and——'

'Does that matter to a boy?' he insisted.

'No, but it matters to a——' she broke off.

'I'm waiting, Brown.'

'To a girl,' she concluded miserably.

'Which you are?'

'Yes.'

'A girl who would have left here without telling me, because she was just a stubborn cuss.'

'You knew already,' she protested, 'you just said so.'

'I knew, but heavens above, I had to be *told*, hadn't I?'

'Why?'

'Why? Because you had to be a woman coming to a man, surely even you can understand that? Why, Brown, you're crying.' His stern voice softened.

'I've wanted to for weeks,' confessed Georgina. 'Women do cry, Mr Roper.'

'My name is Larry. What's yours? I've often wondered.'

'Georgina.'

'Well, you stuck near the truth at least in that. Why did you do it all? Why did you come and stay?'

She wiped her eyes. 'I had to do it, out here is my world.'

'I could tell that,' he nodded, 'even though you tried to leave once.'

'More than once,' she admitted.

'I meant the time you wrote a letter.'

'You took it?' Her eyes widened.

'Yes.'

'I thought it blew away with the wind.'

'It didn't. That was something I still can't understand; you loved it here but you tried to go. You're trying now.'

'I wasn't wanted.'

'*George* wasn't wanted,' he corrected.

'And you're being married.'

'That's true.' A pause. 'When, do you want to say?'

'When?' she asked obediently.

'When are we being married?—Oh, yes, I intended that even before we met,' he grinned at her expression.

'You—you what?'

'Never at any moment have I had any doubts about you, Brown, or about my purposes. Shall I tell you why? Part of my university course was psychology, and that application you wrote me was as plain as the freckled nose on your face. It just screamed Girl.'

'But that was only supposition,' she objected.

'Perhaps,' he nodded, 'but not a girl in a wurlie. I saw you that day you were swimming.'

'You couldn't,' she protested, 'I was under a rock.'

'I saw you. There was,' he grinned, 'a frog sitting on your nose. That was when the game was nearly up. I admired you for your fortitude, and I said: 'I'll give him—her a chance.'

'But how did you come to look in that wurlie?' Georgina demanded.

'Now your stepfather comes into it. You told me he once said that mirages were scenes that were somewhere else and mirrored back to you; I was on the track that day and I saw this mirage—you in a pool.'

'You didn't!' Her cheeks were flaming.

'Why else did I come, then? After that it was so easy to piece together, it was child's play. Your nervousness at our being together, the way you would always shrink away if we were in any way close. Oh, I laughed myself sick often, Brown.'

'I'm glad I amused you,' she said stiffly.

'Yes, but you puzzled me, too. You owed your stepsister something, I gather?'

'Her father's papers,' she told him. 'I wanted them. I wanted to mould them and present them as he would have wished. Joanne would just have sold them for what she could get.'

'Well, she won't be worrying about them now,' he said.

'Are you sad about that? I mean, the money?'

'I'm not rejoicing, but I reckon we'll have enough.'

'You keep on saying "we",' she faltered. 'Are you just baiting me?'

'What do you think?' His eyes smiled.

'I think you could be. After all, I'm no—no—catch.'

'Shall I tell you something, George? Out in the desert I used to lie at night re-designing you. I let your hair grow longer and I put you in a dress. Remember the night of the Min-Min Lights?'

'Always,' she said softly.

'Then you would be shocked, George, at how very near I was to forcing you to change your sex.' His blue eyes were very close to hers now. 'You were two nights on the road with Craig Everson. You'll have to tell me how that happened later ... But tell me now, were you boy or girl then?'

'Girl. But,' at an anger growing in the blue eyes, 'he wasn't a man to me. I mean—— He was helpful, and I liked him. It wasn't till later that I disliked him and I saw how he went through women as Joanne went through men. They should suit each other.' She paused. 'Poor Larry, did he hurt you very much?'

'Hurt me?' he echoed.

'Through Elva and the three girls in the three photos.'

'The harem?' he chuckled. 'No, those photos couldn't hurt because they were my stepsisters. Oh, yes, George, other people beside you are inflicted with steps. My stepmother, of whom I was very fond, brought three young girls with her marriage, and when she died they became my responsibility. Getting them wed was no fun, I can tell you, especially with Everson around, going through each in turn until I finally thew him out. Luckily they all got over it and found someone else and are now living happily ever after . . . I hope.'

'And—Elva?'

'Elva was another Joanne, she was out for what she could get. Craig Everson was attracted to her and took her off my hands, but it didn't last long. Now,' a moment of apparent contemplation, 'what else is there to be said?'

But nothing had been said, Georgina thought. Wasn't he aware of that? Didn't he realise that not once had he told her why he had announced: 'We are being married'? Then what about how she felt, he had not asked her that.

'No, nothing, George,' he agreed blandly, reading her thoughts. Then he looked hard at her, and she knew he was waiting, and being the mighty Roper, he would keep waiting until she gave in.

'Do I always have to be the one to say things?' she burst out at last.

'Well, I can scarcely say "Larry, I love you," can I?' he pointed out.

'Larry, I love you,' she blurted, then she waited for his response.

When it came she was astonished at its sweetness. There

was nothing, she knew in that moment, more wonderful than for a woman to be a woman.

'I love you, Georgina Brown,' said the mighty Roper, and the man took the woman in his arms.

In every issue...

Here's what you'll find:

♥ a complete, full-length romantic novel...illustrated in color.

♥ exotic travel feature...an adventurous visit to a romantic faraway corner of the world.

♥ delightful recipes from around the world...to bring delectable new ideas to your table.

♥ reader's page...your chance to exchange news and views with other Harlequin readers.

♥ other features on a wide variety of interesting subjects.

Start enjoying your own copies of Harlequin magazine immediately by completing the subscription reservation form.

Not sold in stores!

Harlequin Presents...

Harlequin Reader Service
ORDER FORM